www.ChloeEmile.com

Midnight in Montmartre

A French Kiss Romantic Comedy

CHLOE EMILE

This is a work of fiction. Names, characters, organizations, places, events, and incidents are either products of the author's imagination or are used fictitiously. Some locations in Paris are real, and others are fictitious.

MIDNIGHT IN MONTMARTRE Copyright © 2015 by Chloe Emile.
All rights reserved.

ISBN-13: 978-1987859140
ISBN-10: 1987859146

CONTENTS

CHAPTER ONE

*O*n her first night in Paris, it started to rain. As a dark cloud slowly cut into the bright half moon, a few droplets splattered onto Mia Golden's canary-yellow blouse. She only smiled, looking up at the Sacré-Coeur Church.

In photos, the white-domed basilica always reminded her of meringue, something delicious and light as a cloud. With every step up the stairs, she was getting closer, and the church was becoming something solid, something real.

When she reached the top of the stairs, she took her time to visually embrace the church before allowing herself to turn around. She did that sometimes with beautiful places: stared until the image visually burned a permanent place in her memory.

It was close to midnight, and with the wind stirring and the air still heavy with rain, Mia was alone before the Sacré-Coeur, as far as she could tell. As a Seattle native, she was prepared for gray weather, but even as the drops became more abundant, her pink umbrella stayed closed. Instead, she took advantage of the rain, jumping into a small puddle in her rain boots with child-like glee. Knowing that no one was watching, she stopped resisting her urge to dance and sing out loud.

"I'm singin' in the rain. Just singin' in the rain..."

She couldn't carry a tune in a bucket, but she had taken dance lessons as a teen. While not an expert, she could do an impressive two-step, which she did as she danced over to a light pole, slapping her hand on the wet metal and swirling around and around.

The Sacré-Coeur sat on the highest point of the city, on the hill of Montmartre, overlooking the rest of Paris. She didn't get the chance to brace herself for the wonderful skyline, and it nearly took her breath away.

The rain and fog of the night cast a mono-chrome shadow over the cityscape, but it only made it more stunning, recalling the black-and-white photography of old postcards and classic Hollywood movies. A line from one old favorite popped into her mind, and she couldn't help saying it out loud.

"*I remember every detail. The Germans wore gray. You wore blue.*"

It was inevitable that Casablanca would flash into her consciousness on such a night. She loved anything Humphrey Bogart and Ingrid Bergman were in, and she'd watched Casablanca at least a dozen times.

Despite Mia's other reasons for moving to the City of Lights, she was still a woman: she hoped to find love in Paris. A city this gorgeous was better shared. If only she could find her own Bogart. He could wear gray. She could wear blue. They'd have their own Paris, but without the war and the bittersweet ending.

As she took in the view of the city, with the windows lit golden and the charming rooftops with the crooked outlines of chimneys, she searched for the Eiffel Tower. It had to be around somewhere; it was Paris, after all.

Then she saw it, to her far right, almost obscured by a cluster of trees below the Sacré-Coeur. The iconic iron tower stood in the distance, lit up along with the rest of the windows in the city, its tip grazed by the fog.

She looked at her watch: two minutes to midnight. The lights of the Eiffel Tower were supposed to shimmer as if it was New Year's Eve every hour on the hour after sundown. As she waited, she turned back to the church. Admiring the magnificent basilica, she said a little prayer. The Sacré-Coeur meant "the sacred heart," named after the sacred heart of Jesus. Simply being near the divine monument inspired more hope in her both to find her Bogart and to find her sister.

Being here felt like a dream.

When she turned around, the Eiffel Tower began to shimmer. It looked so pretty, twinkling as if clothed in countless stars. Mia had to go and see it up close one day.

"Beautiful. Absolutely beautiful," she whispered.

She sighed dreamily and opened her umbrella. The rain was really starting to pelt down at her. Her hair was in a ponytail, but it would surely frizz up into a puffy Afro as soon as she took the hair elastic out. She started heading back down the stairs.

The wind howled and chafed her cheeks. Who knew Paris could produce such dramatic weather in May?

As she walked down a winding street in Montmartre, a gush of wind produced a harsh rattle of rain on her umbrella. Her skirt was already drenched, but thank goodness for her rain boots.

Despite the darkness and wetness, she still thought the small houses, with leaves and vines climbing up their sides, were idyllic. Montmartre was a neighborhood north of central Paris, and it was said that it was more like a village, with small-town mentality and charm.

A man was walking her way, and it looked as if he was going to walk right into her. The streets were narrow, and Mia stepped to the side to let him pass, but he stopped abruptly to speak to her in a gruff voice.

"*Portefeuille.*"

"*Excusez-moi?*" Mia's knowledge of French was rough. She knew some basic phrases but not enough to know what the man was saying.

"*Portefeuille,*" he enunciated slowly, but just as aggressively. "*Donne-moi ton portefeuille.*"

"I don't speak French," Mia admitted.

The man blinked at her, confused. He was around her age, possibly younger, in his mid-twenties. He hadn't shaved, and his eyes were full of dreary impatience. What was he asking? Porte meant door, right?

"Oh." A realization came to Mia. "Do you mean one of the Métro stations, like Porte Maillot? I'm sorry. I don't know."

"*Portefeuille*," the man cried, even more exasperated this time.

"Really," Mia exclaimed. "*Je ne sais pas*. I have no idea."

Then the man really began to get in her personal space, as if he wasn't close enough already. He grabbed her purse.

"Hey!" Mia pushed him away, but he wouldn't let go.

Her passport was in her purse because she hadn't taken it out after she landed. Plus, there were five hundred euros in there and the only key she had to her apartment. There was no way the scruffy young mugger was getting his hands on her stuff.

"NO! You can't have it. Let go, you—"

The man spat out some expletives of his own, at least that was what Mia assumed. Her French was so bad that she couldn't understand a word. She hadn't even understood his intent to mug her in the first place.

He was really getting rough with her now, pulling her purse with one hand and shoving her backward with the other. Her umbrella dropped with a splash onto the sidewalk.

Mia was athletic, and she took kickboxing classes at her gym in Seattle twice a week. The mugger was scrawny. She could take him. How dare this jerk ruin her first night in Paris?

She was planning on the best way to take him down when the small rumble of an engine was heard and a headlight shone in the mugger's eyes and temporarily blinded him.

This distraction gave Mia the perfect opportunity. She socked him right in the nose, then stuck out her foot and whipped it across the mugger's ankles. He fell sideways. Eyes full of fear, he stumbled to get up. Mia watched him with her arms raised, just in case. As soon as he was on his feet, he ran away.

She turned around. The headlight, now off, had come from a black Vespa. The rider was a handsome man who stared at her with surprise. Dressed in a dark trench coat, he was holding a helmet. He stood closer to a street lamp, and she could see that his dark hair was also drenched, strands curling down toward his amused-looking blue eyes.

He said something to her in French. Perhaps it was to the effect of "Are you okay?"

"*Bonsoir*" was what Mia managed to say back.

He gave her a once-over and smiled in understanding. "American?"

Mia looked down at her rain boots. They were pink with white polka dots. Suddenly she felt like a kid before this elegantly dressed Frenchman.

"Oh, yes, I am," she replied.

He bent down and picked up her umbrella. When he walked closer to hand it back to her, she realized he was a head taller than she was. A gray cashmere scarf was wrapped neatly around his neck. It matched his dark-gray suit beneath the trench coat, which he wore with a crisp white dress shirt and black tie. He looked like the kind of man who would wear expensive cologne. She had the bizarre urge to get closer and smell him.

"Be careful after dark," he said. "You never know who's lurking in these streets, as lovely as the houses around here look."

His English was good. He spoke with a French accent that was more charming than Clouseau-hilarious.

"Thanks for your help," Mia said.

He chuckled. The corners of his eyes crinkled; he had a nice smile.

"I think you took care of it on your own. Nice kick, by the way. Not a bad punch, either."

She laughed back and stuck out her hand. "I'm Mia."

"Luc Deneuve. Nice to meet you."

"Good thing you came when you did, anyhow."

"You're lucky he didn't have a gun or a knife."

"Yes," Mia agreed. "I wasn't thinking. Dangerous, I know. I was purely reacting."

He was still smiling. Her friend Anne in Seattle was wrong. The French did smile.

"What does 'por-teh-fey' mean?" she asked.

"What?" he asked.

"'Por-teh-fey,'" she repeated. "He kept saying that to me."

He looked confused at first, but then realization struck Luc and he started to laugh loudly. "*Portefeuille*. Wallet. It means wallet."

"Oh my gosh. I'm such an idiot. I thought he was asking for directions."

"Like Porte de Clignancourt?"

"Yeah," Mia said between giggles. "I kept telling him I didn't know. I guess he didn't speak English."

They laughed for a good minute. His laughter was infectious, and Mia couldn't stop once she started.

"Are you new to Paris?" he asked when he got a hold of himself.

"Fresh off the plane," she said.

"So you don't speak French."

"I can attempt a few consonants and syllables." She switched to the language in an attempt to say "Hello, it's a beautiful night," which prompted another chuckle from Luc.

Mia eyed the Frenchman with increasing interest. He was not only handsome but also had a good sense of humor and was obviously courageous. He was ready to defend her from assault, not knowing whether the mugger had a weapon on him. Not only that, she liked his friendly blue eyes, and his smile was full of light. It warmed her on such a cold rainy night.

She might have saved herself, but he had saved her from a disastrous first night in Paris.

"How are you liking Paris so far?" he asked. "You know, aside from almost being mugged and assaulted."

"It's been magical so far," she said, looking back at the Sacré-Coeur. "And the experience might've been ruined, except, as luck would have it, you came along."

"Luck," he mused. "I don't know if I believe in luck. I believe we make our own luck, good or bad, with our choices and our decisions. I'm not much for chance or fate."

"Since you're French, are you an existentialist?"

"No." He pointed toward the sky. "I'm not convinced the beauty of the universe is accidental. I'm a romantic. I doubt beauty is a cosmic accident. Whether cosmic beauty or..." He looked at her, then quickly looked away. "Or human beauty."

She blushed as his eyes met hers again. He was still getting pelted by the downpour. If they were in a movie, they would be dancing in the rain. Since they had just met, she resisted the temptation to ask him. After all, she didn't want to scare him off with her crazy and spontaneous ideas, but she had the feeling that if she did ask, he would go along with it.

She stepped closer and raised the umbrella over him. He looked down at her, tilting his head closer, his lips merely inches away as his eyes closed. There was undeniable heat between them. She held her breath. She closed her eyes, bracing for the kiss...

"I almost forgot about the mugger. We should call the police." He staggered backward, out from under the umbrella and back into the rain. He shook his head, frowning, and pulled out his phone from his pants pocket.

"Right," Mia said, dazed. "But is there a point? He's long gone."

"Well, he might not mug anyone for a while. At least not American women." He gave another amused smile as he made a call on his phone. "But we should report him, just in case. Paris is beautiful, but it's like any other city after dark. You have to be careful."

"Yes," Mia said, then muttered, "Life does have a nasty way of intruding into dreams."

Luc didn't hear her because he was speaking rapid-fire French into the phone. When the call ended, he offered to give her a ride home.

Still reeling from his rejection, Mia mumbled a protest. "That's okay, I'm only about four blocks away."

"Who knows what could be in store for you in those four blocks? I insist. Come on." Luc opened up the seat of his scooter and pulled out a second helmet for Mia.

She relented. It was late, and she didn't really want to walk home drenched from head to toe. She gave him the address, and before she knew it, they were in front of her apartment building.

"Thanks." She gave the helmet back to him.

She wanted to say more, but their easygoing rapport from before was gone. They were both acting awkward now, with strained smiles and shy eye contact.

"No problem." He smiled at her again, but the affection in his eyes was replaced with unease. He opened his mouth as if he was going to say something, but he closed it again in silence. His whole body seemed to stiffen, and he gripped the handles on his scooter with more force than he needed to.

"*Bonne soirée*," he said. "Stay safe."

When he rode away into the night, she wondered at his awkward departure. There had definitely been a spark between them, and she was sure that he had been leaning down to kiss her. At the last second, he had drawn back. Why?

Maybe he had a girlfriend. He might even be married. She had not looked at his hand to see if he wore a ring.

She sighed. Perhaps Luc was right about luck. It didn't just drop into your lap. You could make it happen, or you didn't. Luc didn't. Too bad, because in a way, he reminded her of a young Bogie.

CHAPTER TWO

*L*uc took a few deep breaths against the cool wind as he sped down onto Rue Pierre Fontaine.

What was he doing almost kissing a complete stranger? And an American at that. Yes, a cute American, but he had acted so out of character. One minute they were laughing about the wallet misunderstanding, and the next minute he was under her umbrella, wanting to taste her lips.

It was as if she'd cast a spell on him.

"She did have a certain pizzazz about her," he said to himself.

Pizzazz.

It was not a word he used often when conversing with native English speakers. Come to think of it, this was the only time he'd ever used it. It was a word difficult to translate into French. He'd been studying the English language for more than ten years, and he realized that as elegant and melodious as his native tongue was, French was limited in its vocabulary.

English was a hodgepodge language, stealing grammar and words and phrases from every culture as it saw fit. There was a wildness to it, chaotic and exciting. French, and Romance languages in general, had order: rules, structure, a right way and a wrong way. English appeared structured on the surface, but the language seemed to get harder and harder as he advanced in his studies. It was frustrating, given his intellect, but it was also why the language fascinated him to no end.

Yes, *pizzazz* described Mia perfectly. She had the quality in abundance—from his impression of her, anyway. They had only talked for less than half an hour; he didn't really know her. Then why did he feel so at ease with her, as if they'd been friends for ages?

He wondered if Beth had pizzazz. Beth Montaigne, the heiress to the Montaigne Lingerie stores across France. She was the one he was supposed to be in love with. Had he forgotten already?

He had just come from Beth's twenty-seventh birthday party at Le Carmen, an opulent cocktail bar in rococo glory with high ceilings, sculpted columns, and gilded mirrors juxtaposed with modern decor, such as red velvet sofas and golden birdcages hanging from the ceiling, including one big enough for two to sit in.

He'd hoped to spend some private time with Beth in an intimate space or even on the love seat inside the giant birdcage, but she'd spent the evening circulating around the room, leaving every hot-blooded straight man wanting more.

He couldn't blame her for being busy, as there were a lot of business-related guests at the party, and she had her duty, after all, as the face of her family's brand, to schmooze. But at one point in the evening, Luc had thought she spent too long talking and laughing with an Italian business mogul. The man was well dressed, with shiny, pointy shoes and the kind of greasy, black, slicked-back hair that Luc abhorred.

Beth was too good for him. She was too good for most men, since she was, in a word, perfect. With her long blond hair, porcelain skin, and blue-green eyes as bright as gems, she was an angel dropped from the skies. But not only was she beautiful, her intellect, business sense, and upbringing were superior to those of all the other women he knew. She even played the cello and spoke four languages. Above all, she was a nice person. Thoughtful, considerate, generous. She had founded one of her family's charities to fund surgeries for children born with cleft palates. There was simply an indecipherable glow about her. The problem was, everyone else saw it, too.

He'd been chasing after her since they had done their MBAs together. All the other men in the university chased after her, too. She had even dated some of them as Luc watched from the sidelines ruefully, although some of the men's pedigrees, he had to admit, did outshine his. She was a hot commodity, and those who braved rejection were rejected most of the time. Others were too intimidated to take the risk.

Luc, at least, had made some progress. He'd advanced from classmate to acquaintance to friend in her selective social circle. He didn't see her as often as he would've liked, but at least he saw her.

It wasn't the right time, he'd tell himself. Timing. That was the problem, right? Well, there was also the factor of money. Beth had been born into wealth. She had had access to the best of everything in the world since birth. She wouldn't want less in a man.

Luc had spent most of his twenties catching up to his peers. He'd had to work hard for everything. It wasn't as if he was poor, since his father was a successful financial consultant and worked at a top firm in Paris, but his upbringing had been more humble. He certainly had not grown up in bourgeois society, and he had studied his pants off to get into the school Beth attended without trouble, given that she'd had access to the best education all her life.

"Money is a wonderful servant but a terrible master," his father had once told Luc.

Luc had interpreted this advice as meaning he should keep as close an eye on his money as possible. He did so, never spending more than what was necessary. Not that he was afraid to splurge on things like nice suits and a Rolex once he had the means. Those things were necessities that helped him rise to the next level the more successful he became. The point was that he considered each purchase carefully, asking himself if the item or service was going to benefit him beyond its retail value.

Beth had enough money to not even have to look at a price tag before purchasing anything.

Whatever she wanted, she got. She could buy things that were in style for five seconds, and it wouldn't put a dent in her savings. Why would she want a man who couldn't do the same?

However, even though her personal finances weren't a concern, she did have a keen financial sense, and she loved to learn. While her friends went sailing on the French Riviera, she had her nose in a textbook, studying. She knew the business's profit-and-loss statements backward and forward. When her gaze skimmed over the fiscal records, she could spot a financial anomaly in seconds. She had big plans for her family's companies.

That was one of the reasons he respected her. She was also well read, could debate anyone blue about philosophy, and knew more about art history than anyone he knew. Now she was running her family's new company, a sister brand to the lingerie empire that provided most of their fortune.

This was a girl he wanted to marry someday. As soon as his company had that big break-through, they would be on a more equal playing field. What woman would want to marry below her economic level? Such relationships usually didn't work out. The female friends he'd had in college would look down on any man without superior financial credentials.

His company was new, but it doubled its success every year. He could feel himself becoming the man that Beth would want. Already she was flirting with him a little more each time they met. He got the impression that she was at a stage in her life in which she was focused on her career, yet she was weighing her options on the side as to the best man she would eventually choose. Needless to say, she didn't lack for choices. Their social circles were full of guys who would gladly take her off the market.

While he had dated girls throughout his twenties, none of them held a candle to Beth. She was his final destination.

This was the year that his company would be at the top. He would finally make his move with Beth. He'd been dreaming about her for so long.

So what exactly was he doing flirting with an American in the rain in the middle of the night? A tough girl with frizzy hair, questionable fashion sense, and terrible French?

He shook his head, trying to get Mia's smile out of his mind.

Americans smiled too much.

Yet it was a lovely smile, and he couldn't help but smile now just thinking about it.

And her laugh—too loud for French standards but infectious and unapologetic. Free. It had echoed down the quiet street like birdsong.

"Stop it," he said out loud as his Vespa made a turn onto the street of his apartment in the 2nd arrondissement. "I love Beth. I've loved her for years. I bumped into Mia and barely know her. Get a grip."

But he kept thinking about Mia all night. He didn't know what to make of it. What was it about her? Was it the rain and the moonlight? He was a big romantic.

Yes. That would explain it. The atmosphere had something to do with it. It was just a passing moment that they had shared. Two strangers crossing paths then going about their own ways.

There was no denying, however, that she had made him laugh harder than he had in a while.

CHAPTER THREE

*M*ia snuggled under the covers and tried to sleep. It was even worse with her eyes closed. She'd see Luc's soft lips and dreamy eyes lingering over hers, that image frozen in her mind, almost haunting her awake.

She turned on the TV. Juliette had cable, but after flipping through dozens of channels, she settled on *Gone with the Wind* dubbed in French. She'd seen the movie twice already and could follow the plot, if not the words coming out of the actors' mouths. Vivien Leigh's character was a wily one, but Mia had always admired her resilience.

She must've drifted off with the TV on, because she woke up the next morning to a French morning talk show.

Mia had dreamt about Luc all night. In one of the scenes, they were in a field of flowers, where it looked more like Holland than France. He reached out to her with one hand, and she took it. He spun her once, and they were dancing. The sun bathed them in a golden glow as she pressed her head into his chest and they slow danced.

In the next scene they were frolicking as one could only frolic in a dream. He picked a dozen tulips and presented her with the bouquet. As she admired them, he bent down and kissed her.

It was such a lovely dream that when she woke up, she was irritated. Even more so when she remembered that the French stranger not only had not kissed her in real life, he'd left without exchanging contact information. She might never see him again. The thought felt like a punch in the gut.

"Enough of this crazy fantasy," she told herself. "I came to France to find my sister, not to get tied up in some love affair with some guy who doesn't even want me."

She didn't even know anything about him, so why was she obsessing? She shook her head, wondering if she should go back to sleep, but the alarm clock on her cell phone rang. It was a bad idea to sleep for too long if she wanted to get over the time change as soon as possible.

Ten minutes later, she was sipping a rich espresso from Juliette's futuristic-looking coffeemaker and looking out the window. It wasn't raining, but the clouds were puffy and seemed keen on lingering around the sun.

As she admired the view, she wondered what was the bigger fantasy: being with Luc, who clearly had no interest in her, or finding a woman who might not even be her sister.

Somewhere out there in this big city was what she was looking for. She had to keep the faith, but it was hard to block out the doubts.

Through her mother's network of friends in Seattle, Mia had secured herself an apartment in a decent neighborhood in Paris. It was a one-bedroom studio on the fourth floor; the place was small but perfect for her. She even had one rectangular pot of peonies growing outside her living room window. The owner, Juliette, an Irish English professor at a French university, was using her sabbatical to volunteer at an orphanage in Vietnam.

Mia already missed her parents. She'd talked to them as soon as she landed the previous night. They didn't live in the same house in Seattle—she had her own apartment—but at least there she could see them whenever she wanted. Adopted or not, they would always be her parents. They loved her so much and she loved them right back.

Growing up as an adopted biracial child hadn't been a major issue except for the odd insensitive remark. The thing that annoyed her the most, however, was when people touched her hair without asking her. Her hair was a hot topic for many people, prompting curiosity and questions about her background. Mia would explain to those who genuinely wanted to know, but she could feel some people's pity when she told them that she was adopted.

Naturally, she was curious about her roots, like everyone else. Who were her parents? Why did they give her up?

Now there was the chance that she had a sister. If she did, perhaps she'd get closer to the truth.

While her adoptive parents, William and Elena Golden, were both Caucasian—British and Irish-American, respectively—Mia stood out with her curly Afro that never behaved and her café au lait complexion. Her birth mother was African American and her father was white. That was the extent of her knowledge. Mia didn't even know if she really had any long-lost siblings out there. Perhaps it was only wishful thinking...

Five months ago, while watching funny YouTube videos one evening as a way of unwinding after work, she had stumbled across something that struck her eye. In one of the annoying video ads that played before the real video began, Mia noticed a young woman who looked eerily like herself. The commercial was for Fizz, a French soft drink Mia had never heard of before, featuring the famous French rock band Les Slinks in concert at an outdoor music festival. Mia's doppelgänger was just behind the main actor, who was guzzling down a bottle of Fizz in the front row, and she was waving her hands in the air, lip-synching to the French lyrics.

She could've been someone who merely resembled Mia, but the resemblance was uncanny. She had the same kinky hair, even down to the widow's peak hairline. Her eyes were dark and almond shaped, and she had similarly shaped full lips and Mia's high cheek-bones. With the band being French and the concert taking place in Paris, Mia could only deduce that this young woman was French too and possibly living in Paris. Was she an extra, or was she really a fan of Les Slinks?

It was a strange coincidence, too, that YouTube would play a French commercial for a French product that she had no way of accessing in America. Was it a sign?

Mia had watched the Fizz commercial dozens of times since then. Each time she was struck by their resemblance, and her heart would skip a beat. If only the adoption agencies would give her more information. Mia had nothing to go on, and she couldn't exactly knock on every door in Paris to find this woman.

However, she was an experienced journalist with good instincts, and she trusted herself enough to go on a hunch. Was this biracial woman her sister? The answer was in Paris. Whether the answer was favorable or not was another story, but she had to come to the City of Lights to find out.

After doing some research, she found out that LUX, the ad agency that created the commercial, was also based in Paris.

Now that she was here in Paris, first on the agenda was to pay LUX a visit, and that was exactly what she was going to do that morning.

Mia munched on a croissant from the boulangerie downstairs. It was a little hard, since she'd bought it yesterday along with her baguette sandwich, but it gave her some energy. Flaky, buttery energy.

It also gave her some renewal of hope. There was plenty more fatty goodness where that came from. She was in France, a new country; anything was possible.

"You'll be fine," she told herself. "Just take it one step at a time."

Mia had come to Paris with two big suitcases. She still hadn't unpacked everything, but the apartment already felt like home, and she had everything at her disposal to be comfortable for the time being. Juliette had already taken off for Hanoi more than a week ago, but she was gracious enough to have left Mia a welcome basket full of a variety of teas, a small Paris map book, and a list of neighborhood information, as well as a lovely handwritten welcome message on an illustrated card of two lovebirds.

The first step was to go down to the LUX ad agency that had produced the Fizz commercial. In Seattle, her emails to LUX had gone unanswered, and her calls were largely ignored, even when she got a French-speaking friend to speak for her. Nobody knew what she was talking about, and they weren't interested in helping her since she wasn't a big client.

There was only one thing left to do: march into the place and demand answers from someone in charge. Politely, of course, but firmly.

She studied the address of the agency on the map on her laptop. Since she didn't have a French phone plan yet, she couldn't use the GPS on her phone. This was where Juliette's map book came in handy.

The agency was located in the 4th arrondissement. It was walkable. Mia could see the other sights of Paris along the way.

When she stepped out onto the pavement, the gray clouds had left the sun alone for the time being, and the street was illuminated. Mia thought she would be perfectly happy spending the rest of her days in Paris simply walking. She was dressed in a green silk blouse, a mustard-yellow A-line skirt, and brown suede boots. The green of her blouse brought out the green in her hazel eyes. She was usually dressed in a funkier style, but she wanted to look professional for the visit.

The streets were so beautiful, with lush green trees lining the boulevard and sunlight highlighting the blue of the Haussmann buildings' rooftops.

She smiled and said "bonjour" to the pedestrians she passed. Some looked startled, but a few said hello back, and then there were those who looked at her strangely. A few of her friends in Seattle had warned her that the French weren't the friendliest of bunches, but that didn't stop her from being friendly herself. It would help for her to be friendly if she wanted to make friends in this city.

From her impression so far, Paris was as laid back as Seattle. New York and Chicago were noisy, bustling American cities. She was no expert on France, but the Americans had no patience even for microwaving their meals, while the French, it was rumored, took hours to eat dinner. Plus she loved walkable cities. She'd heard that Paris had big, luscious parks that she could spend hours in, and she looked forward to those experiences.

She passed an open market and couldn't help but spend a few minutes strolling through it. It reminded her of the farmers' markets back in the States. The fruits and vegetables, flowers and fish, baguettes and baked goods were all in neat stalls. A vendor was shouting out what sounded like prices for his fruits. She poked through stalls with homemade cheeses and honey and jam. And there were lunch options. Paella, rotisserie chicken, crêpes...

It was only just past ten in the morning, but Mia bought a savory crêpe with ham and cheese. She didn't have curves for nothing. Of course she couldn't survive on buttery pastries and cheese all the time, but the pleasures of Paris were hard to resist, especially for a newcomer.

Her mind flashed back to the handsome French stranger from the night before. It would be nice to be walking with him, taking in the wonders of Paris together. They could visit the Eiffel Tower, the Louvre, the Musée d'Orsay. He would smile that sweet smile and hold her hand...

"Stop it," she said out loud. Too loud; an older gentleman turned around and gave her an odd look. Mia was all teeth as she smiled back and shrugged to convey that she wasn't talking to him.

This Luc guy didn't even ask for your phone number, she told herself silently this time. *He just rode off on that scooter of his, so get him out of your mind.*

After she polished off her crêpe, she consulted her map book again to get back on track to the agency. Without a map, she would've been lost. The Paris streets were not in a straightforward grid system like Seattle's were. The streets intersected and disappeared,

curved and led her astray. Even the arron-
dissements of the city unfolded in the shape
of a snail.

She must've looked like such a tourist with
her head in her map book, but no matter. She
followed the streets carefully, and she was in
front of the LUX agency's headquarters in no
time.

It was a beautiful Haussmann building like
the others she'd been walking past all day,
boasting blue-gray roofs and a light facade
the color of pale butter. The buildings of the
city all seemed to be dressed in uniforms while
allowing small, unique, and intricate details
discernible to those who paid attention.
Different architects had designed them, and
some of them would sign their names on the
building. Mia had read about it in one of her
Paris travel guides. On one of her future walks,
she'd look out for these details. The city was
like a big treasure hunt.

The elevator was occupied, so she walked
up the marble stairs lined with lush maroon
carpeting. On the third floor, she pushed
through the door marked with the company's
logo.

The receptionist looked stern. She was
talking on the phone, and when her eyes met

Mia's, her frown lines got deeper. Even the twisted curls of her blond hair looked hostile.

"*Bonjour,*" Mia said when the receptionist got off the phone. "*Je m'appelle Mia—*"

Her stilted French was interrupted by rapid-fire French. The sharp words seemed to graze her like bullets.

"You're speaking too fast for me," Mia said. "My French is not very good. Do you speak English?"

Another mad gust of French followed. When Mia signaled that she didn't understand, the receptionist pointed to a door the way a general might point to a target.

Mia obliged. Maybe she could find someone in there who spoke English. Why hadn't she taken French at university instead of German? She had heard about the infamous French cold shoulder, but surely not everybody in the city would be this impatient.

She opened the door to what looked like a waiting room. Two women, both brunettes, looking as serious as the receptionist, didn't seem pleased at her entrance. One of them gave her an unimpressed once-over.

"*Bonjour.*" Mia smiled brightly.

The other woman looked down at Mia's boots and rolled her eyes in response.

Mia looked down at them. There was nothing wrong with her boots. They were even designer. Discounted from Marshall's, sure, but designer nonetheless.

Mia had no choice but to sit across from them. Their frostiness could have frozen water into ice in that room.

Still, Mia believed that cold people were just itching to warm up. That was what her mother had always told her, and Mia always felt there was plenty of truth in that statement. The problem was, some people were colder than others.

The women kept sneaking glances at her boots. One of them, the more slender of the two, with small black eyes and a pinched nose, even whispered a few French syllables to the other woman. Mia looked at her boots again. They had a sixties vibe with the chunky heels, and the toes were a bit scuffed, but they were comfortable.

The French girls wore pearls, tasteful blazers, and pencil skirts, with stockings and three-inch heels. Did the people here wear uniforms, too? Mia wouldn't have been surprised.

How long did she have to wait exactly? The receptionist hadn't even known what Mia was here for before sending her in. She doubted the other women would want to help her translate, if they even spoke English. Mia decided to try anyway. What were humiliation and rejection when she had a sister to find?

Mia cleared her throat to get their attention. "*Excusez-moi. Parlez-vous—*"

"English!" It was the receptionist again. She barged in, pointed at Mia, then attempted to speak in English. "You. Go here. Please."

"Oh." Mia didn't know what was happening but decided to obey and go into the other room. At least the receptionist had said *please.*

"He speak English," the receptionist added.

"Okay." Mia cheered up. Finally, someone who would understand her. She could get things sorted out in no time.

The two women looked peeved that she was going ahead of them, but it wasn't as if it was her fault. Mia smiled and shrugged her shoulders at them, but they only responded with more of their icy glares.

They hated her. But she couldn't take it personally. They didn't know her. If they did and they still hated her, Mia would find that to be a problem.

She gave them a little wave before heading to the door the receptionist had pointed to.

When Mia walked into the pristine office, she saw *him* sitting at the desk in an impeccably tailored navy suit.

Luc Deneuve. The handsome stranger from last night.

CHAPTER FOUR

*L*uc nearly spat out his coffee when Mia appeared at the door. She was the last person in the world he expected to see at the office that morning. At first he thought he was imagining things. After all, he had thought about her all night and all morning, and he was sure that he'd been dreaming about her, too.

He was an idiot for not getting her number. What had he been thinking? He also regretted not kissing her.

Under the umbrella, she had looked at him so tenderly, with such a welcoming glint in her eyes and her smile—how could he have not kissed her? In that moment, Mia had been the only girl in the world to him.

44

Until he remembered Beth. It was a confusing situation. How could he have gone from pining after Beth all evening to almost kissing a stranger at midnight?

He had reasoned to himself that it wouldn't have been fair to kiss Mia. Beth might have been out of his league for now, but he didn't want to use someone else who did want him simply to repair his bruised ego.

It hadn't seemed appropriate to kiss Mia at the time, but he also didn't know then how much he was going to regret it until it was too late. There was something about Mia that was special. She was the kind of beautiful that you couldn't capture on camera—her glow, her warmth, her quick wit.

Now she was before him, looking as confused as he was.

"I think there must be some kind of mistake," she said.

Luc frowned. He hoped not. He still didn't believe in fate, but luck was on his side.

"Mia, right?" he asked, even though he knew exactly who she was. "Come on in."

"I had no idea you worked here," Mia said quietly.

She looked shyer than she had before. The girl he had encountered at midnight had been courageous, beating a mugger away before Luc could step in and help. That took guts. Gutsiness wasn't a trait he had considered admiring in a woman before. Shy Mia was also endearing. She looked flustered and vulnerable. He felt the urge to hug her.

"I had no idea you were looking for a job," Luc said.

"I'm not," she said, sounding more sure of herself this time. "I think that's the mistake."

Luc smiled and gestured to the chair facing his desk. "Please, sit down anyway. We'll straighten this out."

She sat, her face illuminated by the light from the window. Her hair was wilder today, tiny dark-brown ringlets unconstrained by the laws of gravity. She wore no makeup as far as he could tell, and light freckles were splattered across her nose. Her lips were a natural rose-mauve, as plump and as kissable as he'd remembered. And her eyes, hazel green, were indescribably beautiful.

The bright colors that she wore were refreshing. Her green shirt brought out the green in her eyes. Her choice in jewelry was certainly unique: pendants in the shape of white cats. All morning he'd sat in interviews with people wearing dreary blacks, grays, and blues until his mood slowly plummeted to match the shades. Just looking at Mia gave him a boost of energy.

But he had to stop staring at her. He shuffled his papers and cleared his throat.

"Our company is hiring a copywriter, somebody with an excellent command of the English language, preferably a native speaker."

"So those people outside were waiting to be interviewed for the position?" Mia asked.

"Maybe. We're hiring for a few different positions, actually."

"Okay." She looked around his office as if she didn't know how she'd gotten there.

"We're an ad agency, if you didn't know," he added.

"I did," Mia said slowly, "but I didn't come here for a job interview."

"Are you here because you're interested in our services?"

"Not exactly."

She seemed to be struggling for words. Luc decided to help her out.

"What do you do in Paris? Are you working here?"

"I'm a journalist, actually. I work for *Seattle Life*, but I'm taking a one-year hiatus to live here, but no, I'm not here to work."

"So you're here for an extended vacation?"

"Sort of." Mia shifted uncomfortably in her chair. He could tell she was struggling with how much she should reveal. "This may sound strange, but I'm looking for a woman who could possibly be my sister. I think she lives in Paris, and that's why I'm here."

Luc digested the information, then said, "Can you tell me more?"

She took a deep breath and gave him a brief rendition of her background. Mia told him about her family in Seattle, how she had been adopted, and how she had come across their Fizz commercial on YouTube, where she noticed a woman who looked eerily like her.

"It sounds pretty silly to say this out loud," Mia said. "In fact, it might even be crazy. I've put my life on hold to chase someone who might not even exist. I know I may be grasping at straws here, but the resemblance between us was so striking. All I want to do is find this woman and find out the truth. If she's not my sister, fine. At least I got to enjoy a year in

Paris. But if she is, I wouldn't even know how to explain how much that would mean to me. I needed to take the chance and find out."

Luc was touched. "I see."

"I tried calling LUX from Seattle, but no one seemed to know anything, or they would transfer me to different people, then never get back to me. I figured since I'm in Paris, I'd come and try to speak to someone in charge. I didn't know it would be you."

She looked at him, imploring, passionate. The fierceness of her gaze caused his heart to skip a beat.

"I'm one of the cofounders of this company," he said.

Mia smiled. "So I am talking to the boss?"

"You are." He smiled back. "If I were in your shoes, I'd probably do the same. I'm sorry you were having trouble getting an answer from my employees. Maybe I can help you."

"You can?"

Luc nodded. "Our company shot the commercial, and we have it on file. We have a screening room where you can view it, and it'll be better than the screen quality on YouTube."

"Thank you." Mia beamed. "That would be extremely helpful."

Ignited by her hopeful smile, Luc punched a few buttons on his desk phone. "Jean?...About nine months ago, we shot a commercial for Fizz featuring Les Slinks, remember that?... I need you to find the video from our catalog and set it up for screening...*merci*." He hung up. "It'll be a few minutes before it's ready," he told Mia.

"Thanks, I really appreciate it, but don't you have other interviews?"

Luc paused. He did, but this was worth more of his time. "Don't worry about it. So, did you plan on working while in Paris, or did you want to take the year off entirely?"

She let out a small laugh. She was becoming more and more at ease in his presence, like the girl he'd met last night.

"To be honest, this trip was a last-minute decision. I do have some savings. I didn't exactly make firm plans, and I figured I could pick up some freelance writing jobs here and there."

"Then why don't you apply for our copywriting position?" Luc asked. "We're making plans to expand our business to both the UK and the United States, and we need more English writers."

"Really?"

To Luc's relief, Mia looked as if she was considering it.

"Our latest project is with a French lingerie company. They want to expand their stores to London first, then other cities in the UK to follow, then America. Since you're a writer, it might be a good fit for you. I'm sure you'd be able to contribute creative ideas. We pay well, the hours are good, and we offer fringe benefits."

Mia slowly nodded. "It sounds like a good opportunity, even though I've never worked in advertising."

"You look like someone who's up for new challenges."

Mia smiled. "I am. But can I think about it?"

"Of course."

After Jean called him back to tell him that the video was ready, Luc escorted her to the screening room, passing the waiting room where a few interviewees—more women dressed in drab, serious colors—smiled and greeted him.

"I know the lead singer of Les Slinks," Luc told Mia as he opened the screening-room door for her. "Are you a fan?"

"I didn't know who they were until I saw the commercial," Mia replied. "I'm not exposed to a lot of French music, but I've bought both of their albums since, so I guess you can say I'm a fan now. Why, are you?"

Luc chuckled. "Yes, we're quite close."

"How come you're close to the lead singer?" Mia asked. "Important businessmen don't always hang out with rock stars, do they?"

Luc chuckled. "This particular rock star is my brother."

"Get out!" Mia laughed. "Are you serious?"

"I wouldn't joke about a thing like this," he said, mock serious. "Yup, Mathieu's about two years younger. He's been making music since he was born, always banging on pots and driving the family crazy."

"That's wild."

"Naturally I was able to convince him to be in this ad. Well, it took a bit of kicking and screaming on his part. He didn't want to sell out, et cetera, but given the state of the music industry, he eventually agreed."

Luc sat down next to Mia and waited for Jean to dim the lights.

"Were all the people in the audience hired extras?" Mia asked. "Or real fans?"

"Real fans," Luc said. "We hired one professional actor for the commercial, but everyone else turned up for the free Slinks concert.

Les Slinks gave away free tickets. The ticket holders automatically had to agree to be in a commercial. It was win-win for everyone."

"Are you able to find out who came to the concert?" Mia asked.

Luc thought about it. "Les Slinks' management gave away tickets at a record store. People only had to line up to get their ticket. Unfortunately, we didn't keep records of who had each ticket. Plus, the tickets were transferable."

"Oh." Her face dropped.

Luc grimaced. He wished he could do more.

"At least the record store was in Paris," he said. "She would've had to come here to get the ticket and attend the concert. Chances are good that she lives here."

"That's true," Mia said.

"It's a long shot, but I can even contact my brother and ask if he and the other members of the band remember anyone who looks like the woman you're looking for."

"That'll be great. Anything would help, really. Thanks so much."

To see the hope back in her expression made him happy. As they sat next to each other, their shoulders touched. Luc felt tempted to wrap his arm around her as if they were at the movies. But right now, being next to her was enough. After all, only yesterday night he had been furious with himself for letting her go.

CHAPTER FIVE

This morning, Luc had been someone Mia was struggling to forget. He'd appeared from the shadows on the streets of Montmartre and slipped away just as quickly, only to linger in her dreams. Now he was offering her a job.

Being in his presence didn't just make her tingle, it was more like a seismic shift. Was that a good quality to have in a boss?

Mia tried to think rationally. She could use the employment. She had enough savings to live on in Paris for half the year. Being the optimist that she was, she had figured she could pitch a few stories about Paris to newspapers and magazines and make the rest of her living that way. But a steady and challenging new job at a French company, where she would be able to make friends and learn the language, not to mention take free French classes, be covered for health care, and earn a decent paycheck, sounded wonderful.

Luc would be a great boss...or would he be a distraction?

"How did you start this company?" she asked.

They were sitting inside the screening room, waiting for Jean to dim the lights and start the video.

"I started LUX with my partner Didier about four years ago," he said.

Mia was impressed. "It's a fairly new company, then. You're doing pretty well."

Luc grinned at her. "Yup. If that persuades you to work for us, we are. And I'm a pretty good boss, if I do say so myself. We also have a pretty great snack table in the employee cafeteria."

"But you're so young," Mia said.

"Don't let this baby face fool you," he said. "I'm in my late forties."

Her jaw dropped. "*What?*"

He laughed. "Just kidding! I'm twenty-eight. My partner Didier is ten years older. He took me under his wing when I worked with him while we were both working at another ad agency. He became sort of like my mentor. I caught on quickly enough that he wanted to go into business with me, and now we're business partners."

"He must've thought you had something special if he decided to leave a stable job to start a new venture with you," Mia said.

"Best decision he ever made," Luc said.

"I see you don't lack confidence." Mia laughed. "How many employees do you have?"

"We have almost thirty employees so far, so we're not so big, but if we do well with our next few campaigns, I have my eye on renting out the office on the floor on top of us. The first year, it was only four of us, so it has been a steady growth. If we win the contracts, we'll definitely need more help and more space in the office."

"You are doing really well, then, if you're constantly growing."

"We could always do better. I have a lot of goals, and I'm not even halfway through them yet. We're not in the top five ad agencies in

Paris. They're in a league of their own, but I'm sure we'll get there."

"I'm sure those companies have been around for decades to build their reputations," Mia said. "You're doing Fizz commercials already, with rock stars, even if one of them is your brother. I have no doubt your company's going to be the top in the country if you keep it up."

Luc broke out into the biggest smile that Mia had ever seen.

"Thanks," he said. "This is why I want you on my team."

"What? To stroke your ego?" she joked.

"Well, yeah."

The lights lowered even more until the room was nearly pitch black. Jean started the video. Mia watched the same commercial with Luc that she'd been replaying for months on her laptop.

"Pause there, Jean," Luc called out. "Zoom in on the woman in red behind the main actor."

Mia watched the freeze frame of her potential sister getting blown up until her face almost filled the entire screen. A rush of emotion flooded Mia's chest. She knew she needed to look at the young woman objective- ly, with a cool, scientific eye.

Good thing Luc was here. His brows furrowed as he scrutinized the screen. He looked at Mia, then back at the screen again.

Mia swallowed as he turned back to her.

"You two do look alike."

"Really?"

"No doubt. You're almost twins, not identical of course, but look, the same eyes, the contours of the face, the hairline, even the amazing smiles—"

Mia blushed. He thought her smile was amazing.

And he had agreed that the woman could be related to her.

She hadn't shown the commercial to her parents, fearing that they'd be hurt to know that she wanted to find her birth parents and possible siblings. Her best friends Anne and Christina in Seattle knew. They also agreed that the woman in the Fizz ad looked like Mia, but the resolution of the video was not the greatest since it was on the Internet. To see it on a big screen the size of an entire wall with crystal-clear images was a different story. She could practically see the woman's pores.

"Mia, are you okay?" Luc asked.

She turned to him. He looked concerned.

Mia was feeling a bit faint. And her internal organs were probably tied into the shape of a bow.

"Oh, yeah. It's just that she looks so much like me, that's really overwhelming."

He took her hand and squeezed it. "It's okay. It must be quite a shock."

At his warm touch, Mia began to relax. Luc had at least two interviewees in the waiting room right now, but helping her with this matter was more important to him. Not to mention that he was the owner of a success-ful company, and his time was precious. That indicated that he had more than a passing interest in her, didn't it?

Then again, Luc had intercepted her mugging when he didn't know her at all. Luc was simply a man who cared about other people. It didn't mean that he had an agenda when it came to Mia. How did she know that a man of his caliber didn't have someone waiting for him at home? There was no ring on his finger, but it was likely that he had a girlfriend. Someone like him could take his pick.

"Thanks for all your help," she said. "I better let you get back to your scheduled appointments."

"No problem." Luc smiled his devastatingly heartbreaking smile. "I'll be sure to talk to my brother and his bandmates for you. I know they're on a tour right now, so I can't say that I'll be able to reach him right away. He goes kind of M.I.A. when he's on tour, but I'll try."

"You've already done more than enough," Mia said, standing up. She looked down shyly. "About the job offer, I think I would like to apply."

"Great, you're hired," Luc said without missing a beat. "I just need you to fill out an application so we can have it on file. In France, we love paperwork."

"Wait, don't you have to think about it? Interview other people first?"

He shrugged. "When opportunity knocks, I take advantage of it. I have a hunch when it comes to employees, and most of the time, I'm right."

"I'm not so sure. You know I don't speak French at all, and you did say you have a lack of English-speaking employees here."

"But I speak English," Luc argued.

"Your receptionist doesn't."

"It doesn't matter. You'll be taking French lessons, and we do have one other

English-speaking employee. You know how I learned English? Being dropped into a semester of university in Utah after I barely scraped by my English exam to get into it. You pick up things fast when you're desperate."

"You're right," Mia said. "And I'm not the kind of person who's afraid of a little humiliation."

"I believe that." Luc laughed. "If you're not afraid of fighting a mugger in the middle of the night alone, what are you afraid of?"

For a moment, Mia panicked. *She* knew what she was afraid of. Maybe working for Luc wasn't such a great idea after all. For one thing, she loved it when he laughed.

CHAPTER SIX

When Mia left the office, Luc wondered whether he made a rash decision in hiring her on the spot. His partner Didier would've been more cautious, scrutinizing resumes and portfolios, checking references, and even going so far as background checks. Luc would have to pretend he had done all that when he told Didier about their new hire.

He had a good feeling about her. Every once in a while, you had to go on a hunch. He had to admit that perhaps he'd been swayed by her on a personal level, too. As talented and efficient as his other employees were, none of them had made him smile in all these years of working for him as much as Mia had in the mere forty minutes they'd spent together that morning.

She was special; anyone would've been able to see that if they spent five minutes with her. Mia was sharp and creative. She was nice, but he could tell she wouldn't stand for any crap. That was exactly the kind of employee he needed at his company.

And her beauty was in a category of its own. Sure, there were some very attractive women in Paris, Beth Montaigne being the epitome of beauty, but he couldn't compare Mia to anyone else. She radiated confidence, comfort in being in her own skin. It was ironic that she didn't know where she came from and was searching for answers.

The fact that she was adopted and was desperately searching for her sister made him a little sad. He couldn't imagine being in a position like that, given that he had grown up in exactly the opposite way: surrounded by family members at every turn. There was always a birthday, anniversary, or other special celebration practically every week, not just with his immediate family but also with his grandparents, cousins, and the like. In short, he'd grown up in a crazy household, with plenty of siblings to spare.

Mia was not the type to welcome pity, and he didn't patronize her, but he did want to do what he could to help her. Surely it was no coincidence that he'd met her last night, then today at the office. His company had made the commercial that had brought her across the world, and she was about to work for him.

Was he starting to believe in fate? He didn't know, but he did feel responsible for her, for her happiness.

He tried calling Mathieu several times, but each time, it went straight to voicemail. Mathieu's phone didn't even ring; it must've been dead. He had probably forgotten to charge the phone or didn't even know where it was. Touring was exciting yet exhausting for Mathieu. The real world didn't exist when he was on tour. Luc expected his messages to go unanswered for some time, unless he got lucky.

Luc called Les Slinks' manager, Jacque. He didn't pick up, either, but at least his phone rang. Luc left a message. Jacque was the responsible one. The other members of the band were hopeless, too, busy with drinking, girls, and god knows what else. Nonetheless, he tried the numbers of all four of them. The calls all went unanswered. They must've been rehearsing or doing TV or radio interviews.

Their schedule was usually jam-packed when they traveled to different cities.

By the time he finished interviewing three other candidates that morning, he only had time for a quick ten-minute lunch in his office, his favorite takeout sushi. After interviewing a few more candidates, all terrible fits for his company, he finally had time to follow up on reading Mia's articles on the *Seattle Life* website, where a majority of her pieces were published.

It didn't take long for him to discover how talented she was. She might have struggled with French, but she certainly had a way with the English language. Her prose was both witty and intelligent.

He was particularly touched by a profile she had written of a bipolar man and the struggles he faced. She wrote pieces on a variety of subjects, both serious and comedic, and her work showed great diversity. The one about the golf fanatic in Seattle who played rain or shine, even a few times during thunderstorms, made him laugh out loud.

Yes, he had definitely made the right decision. Didier was going to agree when Luc showed him Mia's work. He was about to call Didier into his office to discuss their new

English-speaking employee's contract when Jacque called them back.

Luc explained that he wanted to get in touch with Mathieu.

"What can I say, Luc? You know how your brother is. When he's not playing, he's a hermit on the bus, cranking out new songs. His life is music. If he's not performing, he's writing."

Luc knew that too well. It was endearing half the time and incredibly annoying when Mathieu would still belt out conversations in song, a childhood habit. Growing up, Luc had thought Mathieu would have a career on either Broadway or MTV. It didn't surprise him that it was the latter, since Mathieu had taught himself how to play the guitar at thirteen.

"I'm not with them at the moment," Jacque said. "I had to take care of some studio chaos with another band recording in Berlin."

"Where are Les Slinks now?"

"In Chicago."

Les Slinks were promoting their new album, their first English-language album. They had a big following in France and in other Francophone countries with their French albums, but their English album was their way of going international. They were opening for the

Strokes' U.S. tour, which was a big opportunity for them.

"When are you rejoining them on the tour?" Luc asked. "And where?"

"In Philadelphia next week," Jacque said. "If anything, Les Slinks are ending their tour at the end of this month, so he'll be back in Paris by then."

"I know, but I prefer to get a hold of him as soon as possible."

"I'll do my best, but I can't promise anything."

"I understand. Hey, do you remember the Fizz commercial that they shot?"

Luc asked him whether he remembered the girl in the audience, Mia's doppelgänger, and whether he or anyone in the band had talked to her.

"I doubt it," Jacque said. "But why don't you email me her picture? I'll show the guys when I see them."

"Okay. I will, thanks."

Luc hung up. He was going to be a blood-hound and track down this woman in the video no matter what. He had a million things to do at the office, but the only thing that really mattered was helping Mia. She'd looked so luminous against the window's sunlight that morning. His mind drifted to the soft way she looked at him when she smiled, her full lashes grazing her cheeks when she looked down at her lap shyly.

There was so much duality in that woman: tough and sweet, bold and shy. He wanted to get to know her more.

"What's going on with you today?"

A male voice startled Luc out of his reverie.

"Oh, hi, Didier."

Didier was looking at him with an amused expression. He wore round spectacles that reminded Luc of a wise owl and had dark hair that was never out of place. At thirty-eight, he had an air of scholarly intelligence, but beneath the professorial exterior was a man with sharp business sense and keen observation of human nature. He knew what made people tick and why they bought what they did. Together with Luc's creativity, LUX was the ad agency to watch in Paris.

"Are you happy about something?" Didier asked.

"No, why?" Luc said innocently.

"You're sitting there, staring into space, smiling."

"Is it a crime to smile?"

"And you've been humming all day. The employees are starting to talk."

"Are they?"

"They always talk. You have to admit you've been acting strangely. You're practically walking on a cloud. I've been waiting for you to break out in song."

"Humming? I haven't noticed that I was doing that."

"It's bizarre. I've never seen you so... so happy."

Luc chuckled. "You say it like happiness is a bad thing."

"It's not bad, just unusual. You're usually so serious at work, focused. Not that I'm accusing you of being inefficient. You seem to be doing your work at twice the speed. Whatever you're on, I want it."

"It's nothing," Luc protested. "I'm just happy with the way work is going, that's all. I just really like my job sometimes."

Didier scrutinized him with those percep-tive dark eyes of his. "I like coming to work, too, but I don't do a jovial two-step into the office or dance on tables."

"I don't either. This isn't a strip club."

Didier slowly nodded in realization. "It's the Mademoiselle Montaigne campaign, isn't it? You got something big?"

Mademoiselle Montaigne was the new sister lingerie label to Beth's family's famous Madame Montaigne brand. It was younger and edgier, and LUX had been working on coming up with the new label's big campaign for the past couple of weeks. Other agencies were pitching ideas, too, and Luc wanted to make sure that their idea was the one to be chosen. A big campaign like that could catapult LUX to the top.

"Possibly," Luc said vaguely.

Didier smiled knowingly. "Ah. Now I get it. Make the campaign a success and finally get the girl. If your campaign is approved, you'll be working with her closely."

"Who?" Luc asked.

"Beth. Of course."

"Right."

Didier raised an eyebrow. "No need to play dumb with me. I know you've been after Beth for a while."

"Does everybody else in the office know, too?" Luc asked wryly.

"Hey, no need to be defensive. I get it. Beth is the most beautiful woman in Paris. Possibly in the country. Heck, she could win Miss World. No one would blame you for trying to win over a woman like that."

A *woman like that*, Luc thought. What did that even mean anymore?

CHAPTER SEVEN

*L*uc was right. The company really should rent out another floor in the building. Mia had thought her cubicle at *Seattle Life* was small. Here, a cubicle would've been a sanctuary. At least the cushioned panels walled off distractions and gave some semblance of privacy.

At LUX, there were three long tables in a spacious room, and each person carved out a space for him- or herself at a table. Mia wouldn't have minded, since she was a social creature, but her coworkers didn't exactly make her feel welcome. In fact, they all seemed to be giving her the stink eye.

She didn't know whether it was an advantage or not that her table was flush against the wall. On one hand, there was no one giving her the stink eye across from her, but she was also isolated from the others since her back was turned to them. They could see her and what she was doing, and she couldn't see them unless she turned around.

Her new coworkers were probably laughing at her elementary French. In fact, she was sure of it. She saw their faces twitch when she attempted to speak in their native tongue, and she would bet money that they broke out into laughter as soon as she walked away. Mia was even sure that some of the employees understood her but pretended not to.

Sarah had told her that at least four of the employees at the company spoke decent English, but they always spoke French to Mia, even when she started a conversation in English. It was just their way of gaining the upper hand.

At least Mia had Sarah. She was from London, the only other native English speaker at the company. Sarah spoke fluent French, and the others seem to like her fine.

"Don't worry," Sarah said. "It took me a year to raise my French to this level and earn their respect."

"Are the French really that distrusting of foreigners?" Mia asked.

Sarah thought about it. "Only ninety-nine percent of the time." She flashed a big smile. "Just kidding. It's big-city mentality in general. It's a competitive atmosphere, this field. When I was working in London, I wouldn't say it was all rainbows and sunshine either, but at least we had the language and culture in common. The challenge here is to work through those differences and ignore all the office drama."

Sarah had naturally bright red hair and a charming gap between her front teeth. These quirks aside, she was dressed in somber neutrals like everybody else in the company. Mia supposed that was part of fitting in. She had a bright-pink cardigan on over a matching pink-and-white-striped dress. She certainly stood out like a sore thumb in a sea of navy and gray.

Mia didn't even own anything in gray. It wasn't her color. Why were Parisians so averse to wearing color? Was it because they didn't want to compete with the beauty of the city?

Sarah had already brought Mia up to speed as to what the team had come up with so far for the Mademoiselle Montaigne campaign. The copy was originally written in French, and Sarah translated it for Mia.

"Montaigne recently hired Gigi Tom to be the face of the campaign," Sarah said.

Mia gasped. "I love her!" Then she started to laugh. "Really? Gigi? But she's actually cool."

Gigi was a British supermodel who had been on top of the fashion industry for five years now. With her short, punky, platinum-blond hair and a fearless fashion sense that combined crazy vintage pieces with haute couture, Gigi had too much of an edge to be a lingerie model.

"That's what I thought too when I first heard," Sarah said. "But Gigi's very versatile. She does commercial makeup campaigns, then she could turn around and do an avant-garde editorial for *Vogue Italia*. I think the Montaigne company wants their younger brand to be fun and edgy."

"So Gigi's a good fit, then," Mia said.

"Certainly. Madame Montaigne is classical and a bit stuffy. They're going with something different with the younger line, and they need a strong campaign to match so it doesn't get lost in Madame Montaigne's shadow."

"So nothing's really up for muster so far, huh?" Mia said.

"Everything has been rejected by Luc and Didier so far, as far as I know."

"Good," Mia said. "Because some of these are quite terrible. They're not edgy. They're simply sleazy, not to mention just plain dumb."

Sarah laughed. "Don't hold back, Mia. Tell me how you really feel." She looked behind her and used a lower voice. "But really, you're talking ninety percent of advertising. A lot of ad people think they're being creative and innovative, but I agree, most of the time, these ideas are just dumb. The thing is, if you want a campaign to appeal to millions of people, you can't be subtle. You don't want anyone to miss the point."

"Sure, but I've seen some funny, unique ads in my time," Mia said. "I believe you can be creative and come up with something of quality while still appealing to a mass majority. I always like a little humor in ads. Those are the ones that usually stick with you."

Sarah nodded. "That's why Luc is trying to hire more foreigners, so we get a variety of ideas. Plus, the Montaigne company wants to expand to England and America, and the ads need to have an anglophone perspective."

"The American lingerie companies aren't exactly known for being tasteful either," Mia said. "There's a fine line between fun and sleazy when it comes to lingerie advertising."

"Maybe it's better if you just forget about all that's been done before," Sarah said. "The others here are trying too hard to be edgy and unique, and they're coming up with sleazy, peeping Tom–type ads that are too scandalous. But you're on the staff now, Mia. If you don't like the ads, write something better. You're not just here to edit the grammar of the English proposals. Redo the ad completely. You're creative and funny. Come up with an ad that reflects your personality, and that will impress the bosses."

Mia sat back. She tapped her lips with a finger, a habit she had when she was deep in thought. "I've never written an ad campaign. And this is a major ad campaign for a huge company."

Sarah shook her head. "Don't think that way. You know how Luc got started? He was a proofreader at a major ad agency, the top one in the city, in fact. One day he came up with a campaign for a new sports shoe when he was eating lunch. He wrote the idea on a napkin and presented it to the boss. The campaign went viral and he got a huge promotion. If you have it in you, it doesn't matter what position you start from."

"Wow," Mia said. "I didn't know that about Luc."

"He's a genius."

"You don't have the hots for him, do you?" Mia asked.

Sarah giggled. "I have a boyfriend. But every girl in the office thinks he's hot. Who wouldn't? Don't you?"

"Oh." Mia blushed. That was the advantage of having dark skin. Blushing wasn't an issue. "Um, yes. He's certainly...handsome."

Sarah raised an eyebrow at her and was about to say more, but Mia quickly picked up one of the campaign proposals and asked Sarah to translate.

This one was about a masquerade, where every girl was dressed in lingerie, acting sexy, and making out with each other to impress the only man at the party.

"This is terrible," Mia said. "I can definitely do better than this."

CHAPTER EIGHT

*L*uc had it, the perfect campaign for Mademoiselle Montaigne. And it was all thanks to Mia. Excited, he called his secretary, asking her to send Mia into his office.

He saw her every day along with the rest of the employees, but this was the first time since their initial meeting that he'd had a legitimate reason to see her one on one. Not that he didn't try. This was Mia's first week on the job, and Sarah had to train her. He would have trained her himself if he could, but that would look suspect to the other employees; they would think that he was giving her special treatment.

He flipped through Mia's proposal again and smiled. One week on the job and she had already hit it out of the park. Was it beginner's luck, or was she simply as talented as she was beautiful?

Mia knocked on his door.

"Come in," he said.

A twist of the knob and she was in. Dressed in a knitted lime-green dress with lemon-yellow heels, Mia certainly dressed for work with flair. She looked great in bright colors, since they complemented her dark skin tone. Every time he saw her, he felt refreshed, like being awakened when he'd been sleepwalking through his days.

"Morning, Luc. What did you want to see me about?"

He stood up and crossed over to her to kiss her on the cheeks. When he retreated, he was slightly embarrassed by his overt display of affection. Friends gave each other air kisses in France all the time, but it didn't necessarily happen at work. He hoped she didn't consider him to be overstepping any boundaries.

"I read your campaign idea for Montaigne," he said. "It's genius!"

Mia broke out into a big smile. "You really like it?"

"Like it? It's unlike anything I've heard of before. And it's hilarious."

He gestured to a chair for her to sit down, and she did.

"Thank you. I tried to spin a little Americana into the ads."

"How did you come up with it?" Luc asked.

"I was trying to think of something feminine and playful. Lingerie ads featuring models parading around like sex kittens are so overdone. I heard that the company wanted this line to be edgy. Personally, I didn't think that needed to be translated into making the ad even sexier and more provocative."

"That was the major issue I had with the proposals I've read so far too," Luc agreed. "It's difficult not to cross the boundary from sexy to pornography. That's not what the client wants, since Madame Montaigne is so tasteful."

"Right, and these ads are targeted toward young women. What does lingerie do? Gives women a sense of pride and empowerment. Women are intelligent. They want to be respected and feel powerful."

"Power is certainly an overt theme in this pitch," Luc said. "My only concern is whether this idea would go over well in France. Or England. I think men and women would love this concept in America, but Europe is a very different place."

"In some ways, I agree. I know England and France have strict gun control laws, but this ad is tongue in cheek. We're not advocating buying guns. We're still selling lingerie."

"You know, I never dreamed of a lingerie ad featuring guns." Luc laughed.

"Sometimes you have to break new ground," Mia said. "It's a small gun. Bigger than a derringer, but not a Magnum either."

Luc was impressed. "You know your guns."

"Computer research. I'm thinking the guns can even be pink. With the mini-holster as part of the ensemble. They'll look a bit like toy guns, maybe. We'll be able to make our point with humor. I think people will at least be mildly amused by the ad."

"Gigi Tom is tough," Luc said. "I think she'd be good with this concept. She can act, right?"

"I think she's been in a few music videos," Mia said. "I'm thinking the first commercial can be like an action film. Another can be black and white, film noir, and so on."

"Yes." Luc's eyes lit up. "I like the movie theme idea. Wait until the other writers hear about this."

Before he allowed himself to be too excited, he rubbed his chin with one hand and thought about it some more.

"What's wrong?" Mia asked.

"I do have some minor reservations. The gun thing can be controversial. We're not advocating violence; I know that's not your intent, of course. It's more about protection and it's a fun idea, but a gun is a gun."

"We will have to tread carefully on how to go about it," Mia agreed. "You can show it to test groups, right?"

"Yes. We'll need to do that."

"That's good. So you think this idea has potential?"

"Definitely." He clapped his hands, feeling pumped. "First we'll get our team to finish a detailed proposal, then we'll take this to the Montaigne company and get their feedback. We'll take it a step at a time."

Mia beamed. Her smile was so infectious that he smiled back even wider. He hoped he didn't look too Cheshire-cat crazy.

"Great." She stood up, taking this as her cue to go.

"And Mia?"

"Yes?" She turned around.

"I want you at the pitch meeting."

"You mean, with Montaigne?"

"Yes. We'll meet them on Friday in their office."

Mia was quiet for a moment. Luc could tell she was trying to digest the information.

"They're all going to speak French?" Mia asked.

"Probably, considering this is France. But if the Montaigne group wants to make it in anglophone countries, they will have to practice their English once in a while, don't you think?"

"Yes, but will I be speaking?"

"Of course you will. It's your idea, and your English is better."

"Luc, I'm a writer, not a speaker."

"You've never made a speech before?"

"I have, but usually to pitch stories to my editors."

"This is no different," Luc exclaimed. "You'll be doing the same thing. Instead of it being a story for an article, it's a story for a commercial. You don't strike me as the shy type."

"That's true. I'm not shy. But it's been a change to work in France, with a whole new culture with a new set of customs and rules. It's definitely a challenge."

"But it's also exciting, isn't it?" Luc winked at her.

He hoped he didn't look stupid, winking... what was he doing?

"You think the board members will like the idea?" Mia asked, sounding less sure of herself now. "With the gun and everything?"

Luc thought about it for a moment then nodded. "I think so. Sure, some of them will be conservative and might not take to it as quickly, but there are others who are more open-minded. Beth Montaigne is our age, for one thing. Half of her team are women. I'd be surprised if they don't get it. I don't see why they wouldn't find it funny."

CHAPTER NINE

French sounded great when other people spoke it. So why did Mia sound like a choking cat whenever she attempted the language?

She watched the French teacher, Madame Florence, write a phrase on the blackboard. Madame Florence was explaining the verb tenses in French, at least from what Mia could tell. It would've been helpful if Mia understood French so she knew what Madame Florence was saying. That was the whole point of going to French classes in the first place.

She hadn't realized the class would be taught completely in French. It was a catch-22. How was she supposed to learn French in French when she didn't speak French?

"What is she talking about?" Kiko whispered to her.

Kiko was a Japanese housewife who had come to Paris when her husband got transferred here. She spoke perfect English because she had gone to university in Toronto. Mia liked her frankness. To her left sat another of Mia's friends in class. Amanda was an American yoga instructor who also had a biting sense of humor.

"I have no idea," Mia whispered back.

Amanda used her translator app on her smartphone. "*Monsieur Rochelle est né à La Rochelle.*"

"Clever example." Kiko giggled.

Madame Florence turned around and glared in their direction.

"I would learn more French watching that movie, *Gigi*," Amanda said. "Better yet, from Louis Jourdan. He's the quintessential French lover."

Mia tried to suppress her laughter this time. She felt like she was in grade school. She was tempted to pass notes.

"He speaks impeccable English," Mia said. "I doubt you'd learn any French at all."

"We wouldn't need to speak." Amanda was a New Yorker and was quite blunt about her likes and dislikes. As aggressive as she was in daily life, Mia had gone to one of her classes and found it fascinating to see how at peace and swarmi-like Amanda was when she taught yoga.

Mia was glad that she was making more friends in Paris, especially when most of her coworkers were still giving her the cold shoulder no matter how much she smiled and tried to make conversation with them.

As Madame Florence went over the past-tense conjugations for the French verb for "born," Mia wondered if she considered Luc a friend. They had such an easy way of conversing with each other, but a clear line was drawn at work.

He was her boss now, but they had started off as friends, sort of. She was curious about his background. With his manners, his way of dressing, and his high levels of education and success, he could've been an aristocrat.

And who was she? Middle-class family, mixed raced, and adopted. She had no heritage that she knew about, while Luc's probably went back for centuries. His ancestors had probably fought the Hundred Years' War.

If he was from some high-society family, he was certainly not a snob. He was full of humanity and good humor, and those were the main reasons Mia liked him.

Not to mention his blue eyes and the way his *derriere* looked in a suit.

Aside from the differences in their backgrounds, office romance was a disastrous idea. When it didn't work out, they would have no escape. Mia knew from personal experience. She had once dated an editor at *Seattle Life*. Fortunately he was not her editor, but they had to bump into each other in the office all the time or awkwardly share the elevator on occasion. He wasn't a big love on her romantic landscape, but she would've gotten over him a lot sooner if they didn't work in the same building forty to fifty hours a week. Dating someone at work was not an experience Mia cared to repeat.

"*Bonne soirée*," the teacher said at the end of the class. Then she said something about homework. At least she wrote the page numbers of their French grammar exercise book on the board.

"Are you girls hungry?" Kiko asked.

"Starved," Mia said.

Since she went to French class directly from work on Tuesday and Thursday evenings, she only had time for a light snack before class. Even though she was pooped from a long day at LUX, going out for a dinner with the girls would give her a boost in energy.

"Great," Kiko said. "I know this great place around the corner."

***

At a charming French restaurant in the 4th arrondissement, where patrons were already spilled over the sidewalk at the tiny, round terrace tables, Mia, Amanda, and Kiko were able to grab a tiny round table of their own to share.

They took turns ordering in French, then Mia asked the waiter to rate their French.

"All of you were *magnifique*," the handsome waiter said with a flirtatious smile.

"*Merci beaucoup*," Amanda replied, keeping a lingering, seductive gaze on him.

"Subtle," Mia teased her when the waiter left.

"What? I was being nice."

"If that's nice," Kiko said, "I wonder what you're like when you're trying to be sexy."

Amanda laughed. "You don't want to know."

"Since you teach French people yoga," Mia asked, "are they ever mean or condescending to you?"

Amanda shook her head. "No. They're quite friendly. But it's a different atmosphere. People who take yoga classes are more into their health and spirituality. They come because they want to lower their stress. By the end of the class, everybody would be mellowed out."

"Not to mention Amanda is the only person talking during the class," Kiko added.

"That helps."

The girls laughed.

"Why?" Kiko asked Mia. "Are your coworkers still frosty toward you?"

"It's not better, but at least it's not worse."

"What about that scooter-riding, debonair Frenchman who is, in a crazy plot twist, now your boss?" Amanda wiggled her eyebrows for dramatic effect.

"He's still my boss," Mia said. "There's nothing going on between us."

"Not because you don't want it to," Kiko said. "It's such a romantic story how you met. That's certainly something to tell the grandkids."

"What about my story?" Amanda said. "My boyfriend bumped into me on the street. I fell on my butt. My butt was sore for the whole afternoon."

Kiko raised an eyebrow. "Yeah, that certainly beats it."

They laughed again. It felt good for Mia to laugh. Working at the office could be tense, especially when she got the impression that the others wanted her to fail. They knew that her ad had been chosen by Luc and Didier to be pitched, but they had hardly congratulated her.

"I don't know, guys," Mia said. "Luc and I are so different. He's so..."

"What?" Amanda said. "Rich?"

"I don't know. He went to the best schools, and he's probably related to counts and dukes. I'm a girl from Seattle with unmanageable hair."

"Mia!" Amanda exclaimed. "I am ashamed of you. How can you berate yourself like that? You're Mia freakin' Golden, for godsake."

"She's right, you know," Kiko said. "I thought you were confident."

"Confident," Mia repeated, smiling. "I'm Mia Golden. I'm just as educated. There's nothing wrong with my hair, even if it does take up a lot of space and people hate me at concerts. I may not know where I'm from, but I know where I'm going."

"Amen," Amanda said.

The wine and the bread came first. They feasted on the delicious pieces of fresh baguette with butter and clinked their wine glasses.

"Don't let him slip through your fingers," Amanda said. "If it were me, subtlety would not be my middle name."

"It isn't," Mia said.

"He sounds like he likes you. If he's single, just go for it. You're only in Paris for a year. What do you have to lose?"

Mia took another swig from her glass. "Why do you have to be right all the time? Life is short, but I have to find out if Luc actually feels the same about me."

CHAPTER TEN

*L*uc figured Mia would enjoy riding in the company limo to their meeting at the Montaigne headquarters, but he hadn't known she would be this excited.

"You have a TV in here?" she exclaimed, then she flipped through the channels. "And a mini fridge!"

"Don't forget champagne," Didier piped up.

He was already pouring the champagne into three glasses. He handed one each to Luc and Mia.

"It's good luck to celebrate before each meeting," Luc exclaimed. "It's something that Didier and I came up with. We have to celebrate like we already have the contract."

"Does it always work?" Mia asked.

"Most of the time," Didier said.

"When it doesn't, at least we got a glass of champagne in before the meeting," Luc said with a smile.

"Sounds awesome," Mia teased. "Drinking alcohol before big meetings is very professional."

"It's good for the nerves," Didier said.

"It is. You should try it," Luc agreed.

"I didn't say I wouldn't. Cheers."

"One glass only." Luc clinked glasses with Mia and Didier. "We can contain ourselves, you know."

"Let's hope so." Mia laughed.

Luc was sitting next to Mia on the black leather couches. Their arms were touching, and he could smell her perfume. She smelled like lilies, with a hint of something exotic that he couldn't place. It was appropriate that she would wear a perfume that was at once familiar and mysterious.

If Didier weren't here, he would be tempted to kiss her again.

Luc had to contain himself. He had already complimented her on her poppy-colored dress. Her hair was held back with a thin gold headband, and her lips were red to match the dress. Any more comments on the state of her loveliness might cause her to think he was some sort of perverted boss. He didn't want to stare too much or be caught drooling.

In hindsight, he probably should have thought it through before he hired Mia.

Despite her many talents, perhaps he had hired her because he wanted to be close to her. He hadn't realized it when he offered her the job, but now it seemed like it would've been a better idea to just ask her out.

As coworkers, there was a professional boundary that was getting trickier to cross. Mia was a rising star at LUX, and he'd heard that the other employees would not give her the time of day. The truth was, they should be jealous. She had more creativity in her pinkie than his top five employees combined, and the unfair part of it was that it came so naturally to her.

Mia was definitely an asset to his company, but he now realized that he would rather date her.

He chugged down the rest of the champagne. Between Mia and the Mademoiselle Montaigne presentation, he was nervous.

Didier had reservations about Mia's "guns and lingerie" idea. Then again, Didier was on the conservative side, being the rational businessman of their partnership. Luc had stayed in the office one night, weighing the pros and cons of the idea with him. Ultimately, he was able to convince Didier that they should take the risk. It was an outrageous idea, and advertising was all about taking risks. A lingerie campaign was supposed to be provocative, but this campaign would provoke the public in an unexpected way. The goal was to make their ideal customer smile, if not outright laugh out loud. Mia's idea achieved that, and he hoped Beth and her team would agree.

The risks his company had taken so far had all paid off, and they were the fastest-growing ad agency in Paris. He had to continue to trust his own instincts. Mia's idea was brilliant. Surely the Montaigne group had a sense of humor?

Relax, he told himself. *Just relax. Everything's going to be fine.*

He looked at Mia and smiled. Mia smiled back. She didn't seem to be nervous at all, and that calmed him.

She looks like America, Luc suddenly thought. He had traveled extensively throughout the States, notably a summer after his semester at a university in Utah, when he went on a road trip with two of his brothers. He saw small towns, the farms, the famous landmarks. Every city was the same—traffic problems for one—and every city had its own distinct personality.

On a visit to the western states, they'd driven through the Rocky Mountains. The view was majestic, the incredible green mountains carved into the landscape: frightening in a way, yet beautiful. He had wondered how early settlers had ever walked the passes through the mountains in the winter. The weather was lethally cold, and in the summer, unbearably hot.

This stunning landscape was emblematic of the nation. He was a fan of early western movies and had read a few western novels. After seeing the landscape in person, he felt a connection to the people and the country.

Still smiling to himself, he wondered if Mia would feel it was a compliment to be compared to the Rocky Mountains. She should. Mia was wild yet stable. Beautiful but a force to be reckoned with. She had the indomitable American spirit. She was even biracial, representing the nation. And she could throw a mean punch. He suppressed a chuckle. What would have dismayed him in other women only charmed him in Mia.

When the limousine stopped, he took a deep breath. He had to put thoughts of America and Mia—no matter what a fine distraction she was—to the side. Focus on the business. They had an important meeting to conquer. Thoughts of romance had to wait.

He was going to see Beth Montaigne. *Beth.* These thoughts of romance used to be centered on her. He should've been more excited to see her, but he was already excited, because Mia was by his side.

CHAPTER ELEVEN

"It looks like a French boudoir," Mia whispered to Luc when she stepped out of the elevator. "An extra-fancy one. For royalty."

They were on the fifth floor of Montaigne headquarters, and Mia was more than a little nervous, especially after seeing the grandeur of the office. They might as well have been in a palace.

"This building actually used to be the Paris getaway for the princess of Monaco once upon a time," Luc said. "They kept a lot of the artwork and the original moldings."

"Unreal." Mia shook her head. Nothing in Seattle came close to this.

The office had modern furniture: stainless steel tables and black leather chairs. Juxtaposed against the powder-blue wallpaper, the ceiling frescos of cherubs in the clouds, and the crystal chandeliers, the space felt modern and seductive. It was the perfect decor for a classy French lingerie company.

Montaigne was the most popular lingerie brand in the nation. Mia had gone into the flagship store last Saturday afternoon with her French class friends, and they had drooled over the delicate French lace, the silk, the sexy bodices. The price tags made their jaws drop, but they had to admit that it was worth it for a piece of luxury. Kiko had walked away with a pink-and-black silk robe. Amanda had been tempted to get a hot-pink lingerie set, but on her yoga teacher's salary, it wasn't sensible. Mia had her eye on a black lace bra and panty set, but she wanted to save some money from her new job before she went splurging on tiny pieces of fabric.

After Didier spoke to the secretary at the front desk, two French businessmen in black suits as expensive and tailored as Luc's and Didier's came out to greet them. Mia had worn her nicest dress and the only pair of heels she owned, black, which went with everything. She was aware, however, that nearly everything she owned came off a sales rack at Macy's, and her shoes were from T.J. Maxx. Everybody else, even the secretary, seemed to be wearing designer couture from head to toe.

The men escorted them into a room through two golden doors. A beautiful woman who looked like a blond goddess stood up to greet them. She was around Mia's age. However, she was more put together, and she looked as if she had just stepped out of a *Vogue* fashion photo shoot.

"Bonjour" was the only thing Mia understood as the blond beauty kissed Luc and Didier on the cheeks. She and Luc exchanged some more French that Mia couldn't understand before she turned to Mia and introduced herself with a surprisingly firm handshake.

"I'm Beth Montaigne." She spoke English with a sexy French accent. "Mia, I presume?"

"Yes. Nice to meet you."

Mia was surprised. Luc had told her that Beth Montaigne was the young heiress who was in charge of the Mademoiselle Montaigne line, but she had never expected her to be so beautiful. Why wasn't she a model or a celebrity? She looked like someone who would be in the tabloids.

Beth was at least five-ten, and she had a perfectly proportioned figure. Not supermodel skinny, but the type of thin with enough curves to make men drool. Her hair was long and straight, perfectly styled to frame her heart-shaped face. With blue eyes, full lips, skin as creamy as milk, and a neck adorned with diamonds, she was the poster girl of beauty and refinement.

And she was definitely dressed in clothes that were infinitely more expensive than Mia's. A cream Chanel boucle jacket trimmed with black, a perfectly crisp white shirt, and a black tweed pencil skirt—perhaps it was all Chanel. The cost of her outfit alone would probably pay for Mia's entire year's rent in Paris.

"Luc tells me that you've been in Paris for only a few weeks," Beth said. "How are you enjoying our city?"

Luc had talked about her with Beth? Mia wondered if that was a good thing.

"Yes," Mia replied. "I've always wanted to visit. I thought the Eiffel tower was the most beautiful thing I've ever seen, until I saw your office."

Beth laughed graciously. Her laugh was like a music box. Mia watched the other men look at Beth with adoration. Luc was standing behind

Mia, so she couldn't gauge his response to Beth. She was curious whether he was attracted to her, but she also couldn't bear to find out.

"Flattery will get you everywhere," Beth said. "Especially in Paris, where everyone is so keen on being negative."

"Oh, I haven't noticed," Mia said, half joking.

"Please, sit down." Beth gestured toward the seats on one side of the long stainless-steel table.

Mia, Luc, and Didier faced Beth and the other members of the board. Beth introduced each of them. Mia remembered their names quite easily. She'd been trained well as a journalist to remember everything. There were six of them. Two of them were male and in their fifties. Three were women, ranging from late twenties to forties. The last member was a man in his mid-thirties.

Beth turned to her team. "Luc has requested that we speak English for the duration of this meeting. Hope that's not a problem."

"Not at all," Edgard, one of the two older gentlemen, said with a thick French accent. "Shall we get started?"

"Al right." Luc stood up. "I'm sure you've seen dozens of proposals in the past week for the Mademoiselle Montaigne line. Many of them were probably sleazy or outrageous, and not in a good way. How do I know this? Members of my team have come up with these same kinds of ideas. Not to cast a bad shadow on my team, but we as a society have come to expect the same kind of ads for lingerie. Blatant sexuality, the come-hither look, it's all been done before. Considering that Madame Montaigne is all about sensuality and celebrating the woman's body, the younger-sister line should do the same. But younger doesn't equate to being wild and crass. We can still keep the elegance of the Montaigne brand while remaining respectful to women and being fun and edgy, as your team has requested. But instead of trying to explain it, why don't you take a look at a version of our idea yourself."

Luc passed them a file of the mockup ad campaigns that his team had drawn up.

Beth opened up the file first. Mia noticed the expensive gold bracelets adorning her slim wrists. There were two rings on her fingers, but none on her ring finger. It was surprising that some rich mogul hadn't proposed to her already. Or perhaps a few had, and she'd rejected them. Beth was a businesswoman, after all, but Mia wouldn't have been surprised if she had to beat men away with a stick.

Poker faced, Beth passed copies down to the other members on her team.

Adam, the man in his thirties, laughed immediately. Laughter was a good sign. Beth hadn't laughed, though, and her opinion was the one that mattered most.

"'Keep Your Valuables Protected,'" Beth finally said. "Clever slogan."

"Yes," a brunette named Giselle remarked. "It certainly stands out."

"I don't know," Anton, the other older gentleman, said. "We're trying to sell lingerie, not guns. While guns are commonplace in countries like America, in France, we don't use them to sell women's underwear. It can be controversial."

"But controversy's not necessarily a bad thing, Anton," Giselle said. "It's an homage to classic movies, and I think the gun holsters are cute. So much so that I'm tempted to suggest we make them part of the line."

"That's precisely the problem," Anton said. "What's the message we're sending here? That women need guns to protect themselves from the big bad men out there?"

"That's ridiculous," Giselle said. "It's obviously not an antirape campaign. It's still doing what it's supposed to: sell lingerie. Plus, I think it's pretty funny, but I guess, as usual, Anton, you fail to see the humor in the situation."

"Let's put away the boxing gloves," Beth interjected. "Why don't we go over this campaign rationally?"

"You know where I stand," Anton said. "We know what sells lingerie. Sure, this campaign has a degree of creativity, but let's face it. Sex sells. The new lingerie line is sexier, so it makes sense to have a sexy campaign. Now, this is a major international campaign. We can't afford to make any mistakes. The stakes are incredibly high. We want to convince our customers that wearing our lingerie will make them irresistible to men. I'm not at all sure that this campaign conveys that message."

Beth nodded, taking Anton's opinion in. Which worried Mia. She had to speak up.

"With all due respect, women don't always buy lingerie for men."

All heads turned to Mia. It was intimidating in that silent boardroom, but she willed herself to continue.

"When we use these beautiful models for advertising campaigns and turn them into pieces of meat, like so many companies do, we're doing them, and women in general, a huge disservice. Women buy lingerie for the same reasons they buy clothes. When they look good, they feel good. And if they happen to attract attention from the opposite sex, great. But if their main objective in life is to please men, their self-esteem must be in the gutter." Mia looked Beth in the eye. "It's bad enough that society has already conveyed this message loud and clear—that a woman is only as valuable as her looks and her body—so do we have to continue to perpetuate it? We could do something more revolutionary here. We can run a campaign that empowers women without being preachy. It's fun. Giselle is a woman, and she gets it. In fact, she's our target market."

Giselle beamed. "I do. I feel inspired by the ad. It's fresh. It's funny. It's powerful."

"*Power,*" Mia stated. "That's what the gun symbolizes. It's just a symbol. It's about women taking back control."

"Anton," Giselle said. "I doubt that our customers are going to rush out and buy guns because they're in a lingerie ad. Besides, even if they do, you need a license to use guns. They're not easily accessible here in Europe anyway."

"In the States, you have to take classes for gun safety," Mia added. "Although that's beside the point. The point is, women want to feel strong and confident, even if they don't know it yet. A lot of the young women are misguided these days from what's in the media. Victoria's Secret Angels are sexy and fun, but they're missing humor. Women look at those models and think, *they're perfect, and I don't measure up.* You hired Gigi to be the face of your campaign for a reason. She's clever, with unique personal style, and she has a mind of her own. Women don't just relate to her because she's this perfect specimen. They love her because she's sassy and cool for not caring about public opinion. Funny enough, it's what endears her to the public. That's what a Mademoiselle Montaigne girl should be: cool, confident, with a lethal sense of humor. How many men wouldn't find that sexy?"

"A woman with a gun is certainly sexy," Adam said. "I'm a big James Bond fan, and I've always liked the Bond girls who knew how to handle a gun."

"If you put Gigi in a typical lingerie ad," Giselle said, "I agree that we'd be selling her short. Gigi has attitude. She has spunk. She'd be perfect for this idea."

"She's British, but I can tell you that she's extremely popular in the States, too," Mia said. "Americans also love the cool British style. I've seen Mademoiselle Montaigne's designs, and they're definitely suited to a warrior woman rather than a weak plaything. Beth, you're a powerful businesswoman yourself. You own the brand, and you're the line's ideal client. What do you think about it?"

Beth sat back in her chair. She scrutinized the ad for a few seconds. It felt to Mia like hours.

Mia turned to Luc and Didier. They looked as if they were holding their breath, waiting for her decision.

"I had reservations about this campaign at first," Beth said. "You're right, Luc, I've seen too many sleazy campaign proposals, so this one seemed tame in comparison. While I do have the same concerns as Anton with the gun issue, my first impression of the ad was amusement. It's empowering and feminine, without a blatant feminist agenda. It's still sexy. The slogan is tongue in cheek. I get the message that the model is telling the audience that she's in control of her body, and she respects herself." Beth tapped her perfectly manicured fingers on the table as she scrutinized the mock-up ad some more. A smile slowly broke out on her rouged lips. "I like it. It's sexy and edgy, while still being classy. It doesn't exploit women, and I like the pink gun. Well done."

Luc and Didier looked at each other.

Mia digested the information. "You mean..."

"Congratulations," Beth said. "I've chosen your campaign."

CHAPTER TWELVE

*L*uc caught Mia as she lost her balance walking down the steps of the Montaigne building's front entrance.

"Whoa, are you okay?"

His arm automatically wrapped around her waist, steadying her balance. Her head leaned on his left shoulder momentarily, and he could smell the coconut scent of her shampoo.

"My legs suddenly turned into rubber," she said, letting out an embarrassed laugh. "It's like I forgot how to walk."

"It was pretty intense in there," Luc said.

"Maybe I was more nervous than I thought."

"Here we thought you were completely confident," Didier said with a grin.

"You thought I was confident?" She laughed. "I was a ball of nerves on the inside."

"You commanded the room," Luc said, "and got the others into a meaningful discussion. It was impressive."

"Don't worry," Didier added. "Luc and I have made a career out of faking it until we made it."

"I'm probably having postmeeting shell shock," Mia said.

"You definitely hid your nerves well," Luc said. "And won us the campaign. Your speech was amazing."

"Thanks." Mia beamed at him with that beautiful smile of hers that warmed him from the inside. "I think Beth would've approved the ad regardless. She seems to be a woman of good taste and sense."

"She certainly is." Didier gave Luc a knowing look, but Luc ignored it.

"Should we get a drink to celebrate?" Luc cut in before Didier could say anything more about Beth.

"I'd love to," Didier said, "but my wife's been mad at me for working overtime lately. We have a daughter at home who's going through the terrible twos."

"You have a daughter?" Mia said. "What's her name?"

"Lorraine. She sleeps early, so I better get going if I want to see her. You guys have fun. There's a nice cocktail bar down the street."

"I know the one," Luc said.

"Great. I'll take the limo first. Just call the driver when you're ready and he'll come back for you later on."

"*Bonne soirée*," Mia said. "*À demain*."

"Learning a thing or two from those French classes?" Luc teased Mia as Didier waved and got into the car.

"I'll teach you a thing or two," Mia teased back.

When the limo turned the corner, they were alone on the sidewalk. The sun was starting to set, casting a warm glow over them. Luc had the desire to take Mia into his arms and kiss her. Of course he restrained himself. He wasn't sure how Mia would feel about the impromptu gesture.

She was still wobbling a little as they walked to the bar. He didn't know how women could walk in high heels. It must be a challenge. He put his arm around her shoulders to help her balance. At least that wasn't weird. Her skin was soft, but she was starting to get goose bumps as the temperature dropped in the evening.

He took off his suit jacket and draped it around her shoulders.

"Thanks." She smiled up at him. The sun shone behind her like a glowing golden aura.

They went into Pêche 22, a cocktail bar with more than a hundred different kinds of cocktails on the menu.

A waiter showed them to their seats at a round table with a gold stencil of a lace pattern on the surface. The bar was dim, more romantic than Luc remembered. There were couples holding hands all over the place.

It wasn't a bad thing. The waiter came by with a lit candle and placed it in the center of the table.

"Certainly sets the mood," Luc remarked to Mia. Then he wished he hadn't. It was an awkward thing to say. He suddenly felt like his old, gawky teenage self, at a loss for words with a girl he liked.

Mia didn't seem to notice any awkwardness between them. She looked through the expansive list of cocktails and exhaled in amazement. "The options are endless. You've got the Bloody Mary, the Bloody Maurice, the Bloody Henry—everybody in this family is bloody."

Luc chuckled. "I don't know about you, but I think I'm actually going to have some wine."

"That sounds good, as long as the only choice is between red and white."

"Red," Luc and Mia said at the same time, then laughed together.

"I'll tell the waiter," Luc said.

At Luc's request, their waiter, a serious young man with gaunt cheeks and dark eyebrows meeting at a thin point in the middle, came back and poured them the most expensive bottle of red on the menu. Mia deserved it, although since she still didn't speak French all that well, she didn't know how much the bottle cost.

Mia took a sip first.

"What do you think?" Luc asked.

Mia shrugged. "It's good. I mean, it tastes like wine. Why? Are you a wine connoisseur?"

"I wouldn't say that."

"You'd seem the type to know a lot about wine, and you'd be disappointed to know that I don't know anything about it."

"Well, wine is basically grape juice," Luc said, amused. "Have you ever been to a wine tasting?"

"No, have you?"

"Yes. It's pretty funny. Everybody's smelling and swirling, and spitting—"

"Spitting?"

"Oh yeah. Into a little bucket. It's so that they don't get too drunk."

She shook her head. "But that's the whole point of drinking wine."

Luc laughed. He found Mia to be utterly unpretentious and refreshing. He raised his glass.

"You said it. Let's toast to a successful campaign."

"Congratulations," Mia said, "for landing the contract. Were you nervous, too?"

"I was. Those board members are a hard bunch to please."

"Yes, it was intimidating. Everyone's so fancy. I thought I was visiting the queen."

"Yeah, well, most of them grew up wealthy," Luc said. "Beth does come from an aristocratic family. The Montaignes even have a family crest."

"A family crest?" Mia said incredulously. "And here I am, a girl from Seattle who doesn't even know who my parents are."

"Maybe you can create your own family crest," Luc joked.

"Hmm, what would I put on it?" Mia got into the game. "Maybe my spirit animal, the penguin."

"The penguin?"

"They're cute. Oh, and a laptop, since I'm always on it for work. I like symbols of peace, like doves or olives, but maybe that's too cliché."

"I would use something tough and manly," Luc said. "Like a weight set, or a monster truck. Because that's what I am, a manly man."

Mia laughed out loud. "Right. I can tell."

"Anyway, I don't think you should've let those guys make you feel inferior."

"No way," Mia said. "I didn't. Eleanor Roosevelt once said, 'No one can make you feel inferior without your consent.'"

"You're right. You probably made *them* feel inferior."

She giggled as she sipped her wine. "I doubt that."

He picked up his own glass again. "For all their wealth and upper-class sophistication, they're no match for a girl from Seattle. At least not a girl from Seattle like you. So tell me about your family. I'm curious."

"Nothing out of the ordinary. My adoptive parents couldn't have children, so they decided to adopt. I was the only child. Childhood is only interesting to others when there are horror tales to tell, but I don't have many. My parents loved me. They'd take me to Disneyland every year. I never doubted for a moment they loved me and would've loved me no less had I been their child by birth. This is why I feel so guilty that I'm on this search."

"Have you ever talked to them about your birth parents?"

"Yes. They were very open with me. Unfortunately, it was a closed adoption, and they told me all they knew, which isn't much. We started these kinds of discussions when I was about twelve, when I became more and more curious about my background."

"How did you do in school?" Luc asked. "You seem like you'd be a good student."

"I was a good student. Is it that obvious? I was one of those rare kids who actually enjoyed school. My parents believe in education. I always enjoyed English class and writing on my own, so naturally I went on to journalism. I also liked history and became something of a history buff."

"I could've guessed from the Eleanor Roosevelt quote."

Mia laughed. "I can give you quotes galore. The thing about being educated, and, well, colored, is that you draw criticism sometimes. Not from white students so much, but from black students."

"Really?" Luc leaned in.

"Yes. I remember a couple of black students being pretty rude and resentful; they would accuse me of acting white. The funny thing is that they probably didn't know much about the history of black people in America. For example, after the Civil War, slaves were passionate about getting an education. Many of them could not read, and many slaves had to learn how to read secretly. If they were caught, there were severe penalties. Most of them, if not all, wanted the education so they could read the Bible. Many had become religious even as slaves, and they saw the travails as another type of Exodus. Historian Eugene Genovese stated this in his books and—"

She slapped a hand over her mouth. "I'm talking too much. I'm sorry."

"No, it's all right. I always enjoyed history. Keep going."

"I've been talking about myself a lot. Tell me about you. What was your childhood like?"

"Oh, chaotic. Very chaotic. There's seven of us in total."

"You have six siblings?"

Luc nodded. "Four brothers and two sisters. I'm the second oldest. Alain is the oldest, but he's an anthropologist, and he's always off in Africa or some exotic location or other. Then there's Mathieu, who you sort of know."

"The rock star. Of course."

"He's the wild and loud one in the family, along with his twin sister Madeleine. They're both firecrackers. Madeleine also has the creative gene. She's a filmmaker."

"Really?" Mia exclaimed. "French films?"

"Yes. She just got funding to make her first feature, so she's really busy. Actually, most of my family are quite busy. Philippe, the third youngest, is a chef. Xavier is twenty-five. He's a boxer, or trying to be. The youngest is my sister Audrey. The baby of the family."

"You mean, she's actually a baby?"

Luc laughed. "No. She's twenty-two and still a student. She's studying art history."

"It sounds like your family is quite eclectic."

"We all have different interests. That's because my parents are quite different. My dad's the no-nonsense business type, and Mom's a free-spirited painter. Opposites attract. My childhood was loud. Really loud. It was like a circus, almost."

"You didn't live in Paris, did you? The apartments here are not big enough for big families."

"You'd be surprised. There are massive apartments, but you have to be a millionaire. We don't have an apartment. We're lucky enough to have grown up in a house in Montmartre. It's not too far from where you live now. It's cozy, and my parents are still there, along with my sister Audrey. We visit every Sunday, though, if we're all in town."

"Growing up in a large family sounds wonderful," Mia said wistfully.

"There's never a dull moment," Luc agreed, "but at some point, when I was about sixteen, I contemplated becoming a monk in a monastery where everyone had to take a vow of silence."

"Really?"

"Well, not seriously, but I did think about buying a small cabin in the middle of the woods somewhere."

Mia laughed. "How did you get into advertising?"

"Believe it or not, I almost went into astronomy."

"That's totally different."

He nodded. "It is. To get some peace and quiet as a teen, I would go for walks, sometimes at night. You can't always see the stars in Paris, but sometimes you can, when it's really late, really dark, and the sky is clear. I was fascinated by the sky. I'd read books and try to study on my own. We live in an incredibly beautiful galaxy, but at the same time, it's scary how we're just tiny specks in the universe. I still read books on astronomy, and I try to go to the observatory whenever I have the time."

"Why didn't you study astronomy?"

"I realized that I was also creative and had good business sense. Astronomy is not the most well-paying position. I figured if I got into business and advertising, I could be an amateur astronomer, but I couldn't go into astronomy and be an amateur businessman, so I made a decision."

"I think you would've been successful either way," Mia said confidently.

"Thank you." He beamed. The wine was starting to make him feel light-headed, in a good way. He loved Mia's company. He could've talked to her for hours.

And he did.

When they polished off the bottle, it was starting to get late. He wanted to ask Mia if she wanted to eat dinner with him as well, but she made a comment that she had perhaps overdone it with the wine and wanted to go home to rest after an exhausting day. Reluctantly, he asked for the bill.

Mia reached for her wallet.

"You're crazy if you think I'm going to let you pay," Luc said.

"Why not?"

"In France, the man always pays."

"Even if we're coworkers?"

"Yes. You'd be doing us a disservice if you take that away from us."

Mia slowly put her wallet back in her purse. "I wouldn't want to do that, then. Thank you."

Luc used his credit card. He took out his cell phone and called for the car. When they walked out onto the sidewalk, Mia still wasn't doing too well in her heels. They had both had a glass too many, but perhaps Mia was more sensitive to alcohol.

Mia looked up at the sky.

"The stars," she said. "I see them."

Luc looked up. It was impossible to see stars in the downtown core, when the city was all lit up. He didn't know what she was talking about. There were no stars in sight.

"Do you see them?" she asked.

"Well..."

"There." She pointed upward, squinting.

Then she was stumbling, falling back into Luc's arms. He held her, and she turned to look up at him with a sheepish, embarrassed expression. He looked into her beautiful eyes.

For a second they were both frozen in their embrace. He pressed his lips on hers. Her hands wrapped around his neck. He took in her sweet and mysterious fragrance. He lost himself in the kiss, and for a moment, he thought he actually did see stars.

And the ground was shaking. The kiss was a 9.8 on the romantic Richter scale.

Mia pulled back. She took a deep breath. She couldn't meet his eyes.

Then she turned from him and flagged down a cab.

"Taxi!"

The taxi stopped, and Mia quickly ran toward it. She opened the door and slid in.

"I gotta go," Mia said. "Good night, Luc. See you on Monday."

Before he could get a word in and offer the company limo to drive her home, she closed the door. The taxi sped off.

He was confused. He thought they had both enjoyed the kiss. Had he crossed the line?

CHAPTER THIRTEEN

On a sunny Saturday afternoon, Mia strolled through the Luxembourg Gardens in the 6th arrondissement with Kiko and Amanda. They walked past tennis courts, a children's playground, and old men playing pétanque. The vast park featured impressive statues, fountains, perfectly manicured trees, and rectangular patches of grass on which people picnicked and lounged around on blankets.

Mia thought the Luxembourg Gardens should be considered the eighth wonder of the world. The park had been created in 1612 by King Henry IV. How many wars and disasters the world had seen since 1612, yet the beauty of the gardens remained. There was a lesson there somewhere, she thought.

When the trio walked closer to the gardens of the Luxembourg Palace, they decided to take a break and sit down before the round pool, where children were sailing toy boats and guiding them with long wooden sticks.

Mia took a deep breath. She loved this place. Everything in this park was beautiful: the trees, the fresh flowers, the architecture. Everyone from children to seniors found solace here.

Mia could have spent a whole day at the Luxembourg Gardens. A museum was supposed to be around somewhere, as well as a rose garden. Tourists couldn't stop posing for photographs, but there were plenty of well-dressed locals, too, reading French novels or newspapers, enjoying their time off from work. She would definitely come back on her own and take naps on a lazy Sunday in one of the comfy-looking green lounge chairs.

Kiko was hungry, and she came back to the area where they were sitting with a fresh waffle. Amanda was in the middle of talking about her new French boyfriend.

"He's the only Frenchman in the nation who's fanatic about American baseball. He even gets the international channels so he can watch the games. It's so boring. I left America to get away from stuff like baseball."

"If I were you, I'd just go shopping when he watches the games," Kiko said. "Baseball's big in Japan, so I know what you mean. I also had a boyfriend that was obsessed with baseball before I married my husband. Sometimes I was tempted to rip the remote from his hands."

"Did you?" Amanda asked.

Kiko sighed. "So tempting, but I always controlled myself. We did get into a big fight about it once, though. How did a French guy get addicted to American baseball?"

"He spent five years working in Washington," Amanda said. "One day, he was bored and decided to go along with a colleague to see the Washington Nationals, since he'd never been to a baseball game. He discovered he really liked it, and of course he rooted for the Nationals, game after game, because he ended up working and living there. He still has all his shirts and other paraphernalia here. He even bought a Nationals winter jacket."

Amanda looked at Mia, who had been quiet all afternoon. "Are we boring you with all this baseball talk?"

Mia looked up at them. She had been staring into space, thinking about Luc and their kiss...

"No, I'm sorry. Go on."

"Is your guy into baseball too?"

"He's not my guy," Mia said quickly.

Amanda arched an eyebrow. "Did something happen with your boss?"

Mia opened her mouth to protest, but she was bursting to tell someone.

"Last night, we both got a bit tipsy, and we kind of kissed."

"What?" Kiko grinned from ear to ear.

"That's awesome!" Amanda exclaimed.

"No. It's not." Mia explained the circumstances that had led up to the kiss. "We were both high from winning the contract, and we both had a glass of wine too many."

"Remember the old saying," Amanda said. "In vino veritas. In wine, there is truth."

Mia shook her head. "It's so embarrassing. I was the one who fell on him. I don't even remember if I initiated the kiss or not. What if he thinks I'm some pathetic, sex-crazed employee with the hots for the boss? I don't even know how I'm going to show my face at work on Monday."

"Oh, come on, Mia," Kiko said. "Are you sure he didn't kiss you? He likes you and you like him. You're both single. What's the problem?"

"I don't know," Mia said. "It's just that, well, I see him with someone more like him. Someone like Beth."

"Who?"

"Beth Montaigne, the Montaigne lingerie heiress. She's the head of the new label, and I met her yesterday when we did our presentation. The brand hired a British supermodel for the campaign, and she has nothing on Beth. She's lovely, eloquent, educated, and someone I can totally see Luc with."

"Do you think Luc likes her?" Kiko asked.

"The other men couldn't stop staring at Beth. They hung on her every word. I can just see Luc with her, that's all."

"See, you're just making things difficult for yourself," Amanda said. "You're jumping to conclusions that have no facts to support them. Why would it be strange for Luc to like you instead? You're also beautiful, as well as funny and educated. Why compare yourself? Who knows, on Monday, Luc might walk up to you in the office, grab you, and give you a passionate kiss in front of all the employees."

Mia smiled. "Somehow, I doubt that. It's so awkward. I do wonder what he thinks about the whole situation. I kind of freaked out and jumped in a cab after we kissed."

"But why?" Amanda asked.

She shrugged. "My old experiences with my ex from *Seattle Life* came flooding back. I didn't like him nearly as much as I like Luc, but I don't want to put myself in a position where it'll be awkward."

"Where you'll get hurt, you mean." Amanda looked at her with sympathy.

"I know, I know, I'm supposed to be fearless. I'm supposed to be strong. It's the image I project, but sometimes, when you're thrown into a sensitive situation, you can't help but, well, retreat into a corner."

"You've gained your strength back now, haven't you?" Kiko asked. "Why don't you call him?"

"And say what? Sorry for getting drunk and kissing you? Anyway, he hasn't called me."

"Hmmm." Amanda thought about it. "Maybe it is good not to call him for now. You'll see him on Monday anyway. Sometimes guys need space. He'll probably be thinking about you all weekend."

"I hope in a good way," Mia said. "I do really like him."

"Wouldn't it be nice if we could just go up to men and slap the truth out of them?" Kiko said. "What happened to all these romantic Frenchmen I keep hearing about? Is it just a stereotype?"

"In my experience, yes." Amanda laughed. "France is the place of reason, with all those philosophers who advocated logic and rational thinking. French men can be romantic, but they're not swept away by passion as much as you think. Then again, there are those Frenchmen who won't take no for an answer and will call you and follow you around like stalkers."

"You know," Mia said. "Love has little intelligence and reason."

"Men have never been ruled by intelligence or reason," Kiko quipped.

"Well," Amanda said, "to be fair, women are not always the best in those categories either."

CHAPTER FOURTEEN

On a windy Saturday night, Luc sat alone at the counter in his neighborhood bar. He was on a first-name basis with the Albanian owners. The place was kitschy, decorated like a bar from the sixties, or erhaps it hadn't been updated since the sixties. Either way, it was Luc's kind of place. Old men and young hipsters under one roof. Jukebox playing. Cheap beer. A laid-back atmosphere. It was like a time warp, and not very Parisian at all.

His peers, the ones who only knew him on a professional level, probably thought of him as the stuffy type who would unwind over an expensive glass of scotch in a fancy hotel bar. Those who were close to him knew he'd rather spend time in hole-in-the-wall bars. Perhaps it was because there was no pretense in this type of place; he could just be himself and not what society expected him to be.

His bartender Jules was a student at la Sorbonne, where he studied French literature. Jules entertained his patrons at the counter with impressions of his pompous professors and crazy stories about college parties.

Luc chuckled as he listened. His university days had not been so wild. He'd had two girl-friends in his life, each relationship lasting two to three years. He was a monogamous guy by nature and probably one of the last in his circle of friends who believed in true love.

As it happened, he was also the last of his circle of friends to be single. He'd often been accused of being a romantic and for that being the underlying reason he was still single. He didn't agree with that idea. The next time he got into another relationship, he wanted to be sure it was with the right woman.

Not that he lacked choices. A lovely redhead talking to a friend at the end of the bar kept turning around throughout the evening to smile at him. She was undoubtedly beautiful, and he'd seen other men try to talk to her and her brunette friend, to no success. Luc, however, was not interested. Whenever he was focused on a woman, no other mattered to him.

And that woman he was crazy about was Mia.

While he was envious of his pals for having fun on a Saturday night with their girlfriends and wives, it was his choice to be alone. Yes, he did feel lonely, but love was worth it. He was smart enough to know that a fleeting encounter with a pretty girl would not satisfy him in the long run.

For the longest time, he had thought the woman he cared about was Beth, but he found himself less and less concerned about her. When he had seen her at the meeting, she was still the same beautiful blonde he'd known since his MBA days, but somehow his heart didn't go pitter-patter as before. Could he really be over Beth, a woman he had pined over for years, just because Mia had come into his life?

It was different with Mia. He didn't idealize her. She was real. He appreciated her quick wit, her humor, her smile, her generosity. The more he got to know her, the more he liked her. She wasn't afraid to be emotionally open, and he felt as if he knew her well after a few deep and intimate conversations.

And how well did he know Beth? He knew about her. It was different than actually knowing her. He knew she was beautiful, smart, and desired. He knew she was part of elite society. She could speak multiple languages and play the cello. But he didn't recall ever having a deep conversation with her as fulfilling as those he'd had with Mia.

Mia had been so easy to talk to. She saw the humor in everything and wasn't afraid to laugh at herself. She made him feel as if he could be that way, too—honest, easygoing, fun. He liked that he didn't have to pretend to be someone else, someone better, when he was with her.

Yesterday evening, they had kissed. It had been an accidental kiss, prompted by wine, but it had been the best kiss he'd ever had. Now that he'd kissed her, he knew why he had felt regret before, during the night of Mia's mugging in Montmartre, when he'd squandered the chance.

The problem was, she was still his employee. An employee/boss relationship was fraught with professional and emotional risks. It didn't matter to him so much what the employees thought about him, but Mia was already despised at the office. What if nasty rumors spread about her being the boss's favorite for reasons other than her talent and professionalism?

Not that they had done anything, really. It was all theoretical, but what if the others thought she got her job because she used her sexuality to get cozy with the boss? He had hired her on the spot, after all. At least a couple of the employees knew that, the ones in HR.

He would never want to be responsible for tainting Mia's reputation. While she was charming enough to tempt any man, she would never behave unethically. She had the highest integrity.

Which was probably why she had left so abruptly after they kissed.

Luc sighed.

"Anything else, *monsieur*?" Jules the bartender asked.

Luc looked down. His glass was empty.

"I'll have another," he said.

"Woman problems?" Jules looked at him knowingly. Which was funny to Luc because Jules was probably still in his teens.

"To a degree," Luc admitted. "A woman problem is a nice problem to have, if you can just work out the details."

"Maybe." Jules placed the new glass in front of Luc and took away the empty one. "The only men without women problems are those who are gay or dead."

Luc laughed. "Well, I'm not gay, and I'm not dead yet."

"If you really want her, get her." Jules took out his iPhone and showed Luc photos of his cute girlfriend from his Instagram. "My girlfriend Adelle. I was in love with her the moment I saw her walking across campus. It took me months to win her over. If you want her, nothing should get in the way." Jules raised his glass. "Cheers."

"Cheers," Luc said. "You're right. You're young but wise, my man."

He liked Mia, and she seemed to like him. If she didn't, she wouldn't have kissed him back so passionately. Who cared what the other employees thought? There was something between them, and he wasn't going to let other people's opinions, or his own pride, get in the way.

On Monday, when he saw her, he would tell her how he felt about her.

CHAPTER FIFTEEN

*M*ia had spent most of the weekend thinking about Luc. She couldn't help it. She looked forward to Monday morning when she'd get to see him again, yet she also dreaded it, fearing what he was going to say or not say.

How would he treat her? Would he acknowledge that steamy moment outside the bar, or would he pretend nothing had happened?

He hadn't called her all weekend. What if he was embarrassed by the kiss or was even disgusted by it?

When she went into the office, she was surprised to find a few coworkers responding to her morning greetings with friendlier attitudes.

"Congratulations on the campaign," one guy said, in English no less.

No one in the office, aside from Sarah, Luc, and Didier, had ever said a kind word to her. They usually replied to her cheerful words begrudgingly and gave her stony looks of disinterest.

When Mia approached her desk, Sarah gave her a hug as soon as she saw her. "I knew it! I knew they'd pick your campaign. Well done."

"Thanks," Mia said brightly.

"Some of the people here are dying with envy, but the others are forming newfound respect for you."

"You really do have to earn your place here." Mia told her about the warm reception she had received that morning.

"No kidding. See? I told you they'd come around."

"Hey, has Luc been in yet?"

Sarah shook her head. "Don't think so. At least, I haven't seen him in yet."

Mia breathed a sigh of relief. She'd been tense knowing that she could run into Luc at any moment; she would have to speak to him

142

sooner or later. Although she was in the clear for now, a part of her did want the meeting to happen sooner to get the awkwardness out of the way.

When he came, it should be easy to find an excuse to talk to him. She could ask him questions about the Montaigne campaign. What were they going to run first, magazine or TV ads? Which publications or stations? Would the ads run in France first or in the UK simultaneously? Any of those questions were valid. She did want to know the answers, as they were related to her work.

It would also be nice if he could answer questions of a romantic nature as well.

Such as: Do you love me?

Mia groaned to herself. She would never ask that. Not in a million years.

But she did want to know whether he was interested in her. He was so nice to her, going above and beyond to help her both profession-ally and personally. She didn't want to misread the signs or take advantage of his generosity.

Or what if she didn't misread him? What if he did calm all her fears with another passion-ate kiss in his office? His strong arms wrapped around her, her chest feeling the heat of his body, his lips all over her—

Stop it, she told herself.

She shuffled through the papers on her desk as a way of distracting herself from her thoughts.

"Mia, *bonjour.*"

Mia looked up. A French woman, about twenty-five with a platinum-blond bob, was standing over her, smiling.

"*Bonjour,*" Mia replied. She recognized the coworker as one of the graphic designers. She'd seen her look at her with curiosity from time to time in passing, but they hadn't had the opportunity to speak.

"I just wanted to say that I heard about the Montaigne campaign and thought your idea was excellent," the woman said in heavily accented English. "I'm Amélie, by the way."

"Thank you," Mia said, smiling back.

"I'm glad it was approved." Amélie paused. "Please excuse my English. It must be terrible."

Amélie looked so stressed that Mia felt a wave of sympathy. "You're joking, right? Your English is way better than my French. *Mon francais est horrible.*"

Amélie laughed. "*Non.* It's fine. I can understand what you're saying."

"Even if my accent is as thick as molasses?" Mia gestured to Sarah's empty chair. "Please, sit for a moment. Can I ask you something?"

"Sure," Amélie said as she eased into the chair.

"I got the feeling that I wasn't exactly well liked in the office. Most of the people here were Arctic ice cold. Is the glacier starting to melt?"

Amélie sighed. "There's definitely some—what would you call it in English—office politics? You know Brigette, in HR? Brigette has been working here the longest. And Lina's practically her sidekick. She's been here almost as long. What they say goes around here."

"So they're like the queen bees here," Mia said. "I feel like I'm in high school again. Their opinions really matter in this professional work environment?"

"Unfortunately, yes. If they form an opinion of you, it takes a while for them to change it. The others like to be on their good side. I should've ignored 'the orders' from the start. I was a bit insecure and barely getting along with them myself, since I only started working here five months ago. I was nervous for my job, but I should've stood up to them."

"It's okay. Thanks for letting me know. I thought it was strange that everyone just decided I was invisible from the start."

"I know. It's terrible. I felt really bad when I saw them treating you this way. It took me too long to talk to you."

"It's really all right," Mia said. "It's hard to get in the middle of office dramas. Hey, I noticed a couple of people actually being friendly this morning."

"A few of us have talked about it, and we're tired of Brigette and Lina's tyrannical behavior. There's no reason not to give you a chance. Now that you've won a campaign that had been a challenge for everyone at LUX, including the bosses, people are starting to see that you are an asset to the company, and that Brigette and Lina are wrong."

"I really don't bite," Mia said. "I think they would like me if they got to know me."

"I know. You seem so friendly, and I regret not talking to you sooner."

"Better late than never. I really appreciate it anyway."

"I guess we'll be working together more, since I'll be working on the Montaigne magazine ads." Amélie stood up. "I better get back."

"Thanks," Mia said. "I'll see you around."

Amélie turned around.

"I know it's petty, but it's not personal. It's jealousy. In fact, I think they're insecure about their jobs, and they feel threatened by anybody who's new."

Amélie went back to the table where the designers worked. Mia turned around and caught Brigette's eye. Brigette gave Mia one of her usual frosty looks and went back to talking to Lina.

Mia shrugged. There were some people in the world who simply didn't like you due to their own insecurities. What could she do? All Mia could focus on were the people who did appreciate her.

She got up to get some coffee from the break room. She focused on the positives so far: at least a few other employees were warming up to her. Her Monday was off to a good start.

In the break room, Didier was making an espresso.

"Good morning, Mia," he said over the noise of the machine. "Congratulations again on the campaign. We're all excited to start working on it."

"Fingers crossed that the public will like it," Mia replied.

"Who knows what will appeal to the public? It's always a surprise, but it would really surprise me if your campaign isn't well received. Luc seems confident that it'll do well. I trust him. He's a lot better at predicting public response than I am."

"Speaking of Luc, is he in yet?"

"Not yet. If he was, you'd know it. He'd be humming to himself with his head in the clouds, with that silly grin on his face. Have you noticed?"

"That he's happy?" Mia said. "I thought that was what he was like."

"No. He's usually much more serious. He's only been this cheerful in the past few weeks."

"So what's gotten into him?"

Didier grinned. At first Mia thought he was going to say it was because of her, and she looked away shyly.

"Probably because of Beth Montaigne."

Mia looked up, startled. "Beth?" she said weakly.

"Luc will be working with her more closely now that he has the Mademoiselle Montaigne campaign. He's been in love with her for years.

Didn't you see how excited he was after Beth approved the ad?"

"Yes, I suppose…"

"Now this will finally be his chance to win her over. Working on the campaign will throw them together, and he'll finally be weeded out from the pack of suitors that's always surrounding her."

Mia felt nauseated. It was as if she'd been hit with a tranquilizer in the heart. Her hand shook as she put her espresso cup in the machine when Didier was finished with it.

"I didn't know that Luc liked Beth," she said as normally as she could while conjuring up a fake smile.

"Oh yes. They did their MBAs together. He's been carrying a torch big enough to ignite a forest. But can you blame the man? She could walk into a room and turn gay men straight. Beth is not like most women. She's beautiful and rich but also ambitious. She's determined to be respected for her business skills, too, and be admired for her brains on top of her beauty. Most women of her status would live off their looks and family, so that's very admirable. She's picky, that one. If she picks Luc, he'd win the prize of a lifetime."

Mia turned on the espresso machine, letting the cat-gargling noise silence the breaking of her heart.

"Absolutely," Mia said. "I can't blame him either."

Didier poked his head out the door. "Oh, I see Luc coming in. I'm going to have a quick chat with him first. Enjoy your *café*."

"Thanks. See you."

Mia gulped the bitter liquid. It burned its way down her throat.

And her cheeks burned. So did her heart. Everything in her body seemed to be on fire.

How was she supposed to face Luc now? He'd been in love with Beth all this time, and she got drunk and threw herself at him. It was mortifying.

Someone like Beth Montaigne would never do something like that.

She sat down at the empty round table in the middle of the break room and contemplated what she was going to do when she saw him. Before she could decide, however, Luc poked his head into the break room.

"Mia?"

She almost jumped out of her seat. At least the espresso cup raised up to her lips was empty, so she didn't spill anything.

"Oh, I'm sorry," Luc said. "I didn't mean to startle you. Didier said you were here, and I wanted to talk to you."

He still had his coat on, and he was carrying a mahogany briefcase with his initials on it. She couldn't look into his eyes for long.

"Sure."

"Come into my office."

She followed him as he opened the door and turned the lights on. Even though she'd been in his office before, this time the room felt sterile and cold. The desk was made of glass, and the chairs were stainless steel and black leather. It was classic, sleek, and modern, like the male version of Beth's office. Mia had the urge to run out of there.

He closed the door behind them. She sat down while he went around to sit behind his desk.

"I wanted to talk to you about Friday night," he said slowly.

Luc looked uncomfortable. What if he wanted to reprimand her or even fire her?

If she'd known he had the hots for Beth, she wouldn't have been so careless.

He opened his mouth to speak again, looking as if he was choosing his words carefully.

"I–"

"I'm really upset about what happened, too," she blurted out. "We're both professionals, and I shouldn't have gotten drunk enough to do something utterly regrettable. We were caught up in the excitement, with the campaign and everything. It was just one too many drinks. I'm so sorry. I just want to be clear that it was nothing but a misunderstanding."

"Oh." Luc looked surprised. He was silent for a moment.

Mia braced herself. She looked away.

"Okay," he said slowly. "I'm glad we got that sorted out."

"Let's just forget it ever happened," Mia said. "I'm very good, you know, at forgetting things."

"Really?" Luc looked at her with a serious expression. "The history buff?"

Mia gulped. "I remember what I want to remember, and I can let go of the rest. Free the brain up for what's important, right?"

"Right." His voice was grave. "I guess you've said all there is to say."

"No hard feelings?"

"None." His smile was bittersweet. "We have a lot of work to do on the campaign, and we've gotten along professionally so far. I'm sorry if I have offended you—"

"No, no," Mia protested. "It was entirely my fault. You were a gentleman. Again, I'm really sorry." She got up. "Well, I should get back to my desk and start working. I'm sure you have a lot to catch up with this morning."

"Okay." He gave her a strange look.

She scurried to the door, not wanting to spend another second in that room with him, with the rejection of the whole humiliating situation.

She went back into the break room to make herself another espresso.

"I need something stronger than this," she muttered.

CHAPTER SIXTEEN

When Mia left Luc's office, his tie felt too tight, choking into his skin. His neck itched. He grabbed at the knot and pulled it away from his neck, but even with the tie loosened, he still felt as if he was being choked.

He realized that his whole body had tensed up. It was probably its way of forming a big, heavy scab around his heart.

Luc was at least thankful that he'd been sitting down when Mia crushed him with her sharp words. At least he couldn't keel over while sitting in a heavy, industry-standard office chair.

The world really did revolve around women. They could build a man or destroy him. When he had awakened that morning, he hadn't expected the rejection to be so brutal. He hadn't expected rejection, period. His future with Mia had been so clear to him.

He had been planning on asking her out on a real date. He would've cooked for her, taken her out to a park for a picnic, perhaps along the Seine River, at the Tuileries, or Luxembourg Gardens. Something easygoing yet romantic, so they could talk and get to know each other even more.

The first date would lead to the second date and the second date the third. He could see them falling in love, moving in together. She'd move to Paris to be with him permanently because he would propose...

Perhaps he had really gotten ahead of himself. When was he going to learn to separate fantasy from reality?

Now that he knew how Mia really felt about the kiss, he was glad that he'd restrained himself from calling her during the weekend.

"*I remember what I want to remember, and I can let go of the rest,*" she had said.

If only he could pick and choose what he wanted to remember, he wouldn't feel this wretched.

It turned out that he was the only one who felt it. The kiss.

Their kiss had been more than just lips meeting. It was lyrical and passionate and sexy at the same time. He couldn't just walk away from that.

But apparently Mia could.

"You look so serious, Luc. Who died?"

A woman's teasing voice. Not Mia's.

He looked up. Beth was at the door, the light from the hallway casting a perfect silhouette of her svelte body.

"Hope I'm not interrupting." She smiled.

Luc overcame his surprise quickly and stood up. "No, of course not. Come on in."

She closed the door behind her, and he greeted her with air kisses on the cheeks. She looked stunning as always in a tight baby-blue dress with silver swirling down the bodice at an angle, reminding him of a tornado. Her blond hair was styled in waves, framing her porcelain face. She wore dark red lipstick, a bold, sexy shade that he hadn't seen on her before.

"Did you get some bad news, Luc? The stock market down? You're really wearing a funeral parlor face, you know."

Luc shook his head. "Sorry, I was just thinking about our campaigns."

She arched an eyebrow. "About what could go wrong? You worry too much, Luc."

"It's just a case of the Mondays." He mustered a smile, hoping it would convince her. "What brings me the pleasure of seeing you this morning?"

Beth took out a folder from her tan Hérmes handbag. "I just wanted to bring you these, the contracts we have to get signed."

Luc took them and went back to sit at his desk.

"You came out all the way for that? You could've sent a messenger, you know."

He dropped the folder in front of him and was about to ask Beth to sit in the seat where Mia had just sat when Beth coolly strutted over to his side of the desk. She leaned over him, and he could smell her seductive perfume. In the past, a whiff of Beth's deadly drop of expensive perfume would've sent him into raptures, but this time, it had little effect on him, strangely enough.

"I just wanted to say hello," Beth said coyly.

He opened the folder and looked over the contracts in silence.

"Nothing has changed since we last talked," Beth said. "We're just making this official and legal."

Luc grabbed a pen and signed his name on several pages.

"Here you go." Luc closed the folder and gave it back to Beth.

She looked perplexed for a moment, but a smile reappeared on her face just as quickly. Perhaps she wasn't used to Luc being this silent. Usually he was the one struggling to make conversation.

"Are you working on the campaign this morning?" Beth asked.

"Yes. We're all working on our parts individually, and we're going to meet this afternoon to go over everything, Didier, Mia, and I."

He cringed when he said Mia's name.

"Oh, is that the American girl who came to the pitch meeting?" Beth asked. "Mia?"

"Yes," he said, looking back down at his desk, which was now empty.

"Mia. She was a firecracker. I was hesitant about the campaign at first, but her speech convinced me in the end. Which ad agency did she work for in America?"

"Actually, she was a journalist at *Seattle Life* magazine. She's just a natural at this advertising stuff."

"She certainly got lucky, if this is her first big campaign. Where did you find her?"

"On a street in Montmartre."

Beth raised an eyebrow. There were unsavory parts of Montmartre, such as Pigalle, which was full of sex shows and seedy bars.

"All innocent, of course," Luc quickly explained. He told her the full story, of how he'd been riding his scooter home late at night and saw Mia fighting off a mugger.

Beth was amused by the incident. "So you felt sorry enough for her to offer her a job?"

"Oh. That's another long story. Long story short, Mia came into my office the next morning because she had to track down someone in one of the commercials our company made for personal reasons. The funny thing is, she didn't know I worked here. I was in the process of interviewing candidates for an English-speaking copywriting position for the company. Since Mia has plenty of writing experience, I thought it would be a good fit for her to work for us."

"And you were right," Beth said. "As always. That's quite a serendipitous meeting."

"Yes. Quite a way for her to meet her future boss."

Casually, Beth sat on his desk. She crossed her legs, allowing her dress to hike up and expose her creamy thighs.

"I'm so happy that we'll be working on this campaign together," Beth said. "We're both so busy that we rarely get to spend time together."

"We saw each other at your birthday party," Luc said.

"Yes, but I don't recall getting much time with you, since there were so many guests. That can change now."

Her syllables and consonants were wrapped in an aroma of sexual tenderness. She'd never expressed an interest in spending time alone with him before. He should've been ecstatic. She looked good, she smelled good, and she was saying all the things he'd been waiting to hear, so why didn't he feel anything?

She shifted her top leg. The dress inched up even higher.

"Have you been working out, Luc?"

"Not really. I haven't had time to go to the gym at all."

"That's strange, because you look more fit than usual. Whatever you're doing, keep it up."

Was Beth trying to seduce him right here in his office? He'd seen her turn on the charm and get flirty with men she was interested in before, but he'd never experienced it himself. A mixture of emotions swirled in his brain. In the past, he wouldn't have hesitated to take the bait, but he was too upset about Mia.

"Is something wrong, Luc? You seem really distracted today."

Luc shook his head. "Sorry. I didn't get much sleep last night."

"That's all right," she said, but her voice deflated in disappointment. "This business can give me a few sleepless nights too. Drink a glass of wine if you ever feel that way. It helps me. I do envy those people who are out like a light as soon as their head hits the pillow." She cocked her head at him. "Maybe you need someone to sleep with. That might be better than a glass of wine."

Her red lips spread into a mischievous smile. Luc had never known she could be so bold. Then again, Beth was the kind of woman who liked to get what she wanted and who had the power to do so.

If only she had wanted him before he met Mia.

"Maybe," he said vaguely.

Beth uncrossed her legs and frowned. She cocked her head at him again.

"Luc, why don't we have dinner tonight? It'll help get you out of whatever funk you're in."

"Dinner?" Luc looked up at her.

"Sure. As old friends and new business partners. We should celebrate."

"Oh. Sure," Luc said slowly. "That could be fun."

Luc just wanted to be alone at the moment. Luckily, Beth was standing up and picking up her bag from the table, ready to leave.

"Pick me up at eight?" she asked.

"Sure."

"How about Chez Antoine?"

"Sounds good." He mustered another smile. "See you then."

Beth smiled back, but she looked at him strangely. Perhaps she wasn't used to Luc being distracted. She was usually the one causing the distractions. He had always given her his undivided attention in the past. It was a bit strange that he wasn't jumping for joy that Beth had asked *him* out for dinner.

It did sound fun, sort of, if they were going out to celebrate the campaign as friends. But his gut feeling told him that it was a date.

A date with Beth. Even a month ago, that would've felt like winning the lottery. In fact, he had believed that he had a better chance of winning the lottery than going out on a real date with Beth Montaigne. Now the chance had fallen right into his lap without him doing anything. It happened so quickly, so easily.

Maybe it wasn't such a bad thing to date Beth. Not at all.

After all, Mia wasn't interested in going out with him. And the most desired woman in Paris was.

CHAPTER SEVENTEEN

*A*rt was a wonderful thing to take your mind off troubles...and men. Although oftentimes men were the trouble. Mia strolled through the gardens of the Rodin Museum, relieved that the gray clouds had dispersed and the sun was peeking out, illuminating the beautiful red and yellow roses in their glory among Rodin's powerful sculptures.

She was grateful for the beautiful distractions, the peaceful afternoon alone, and the wonderful spring weather that accompanied them. In these moments, she felt like Paris was really her own.

Rodin had been really prolific, she thought as she gazed at a sculpture of a male torso. Being prolific was something that might have been held against him in the United States. Authors who were prolific were often looked upon with suspicion. Eyebrows raised with sculptors, too. Many didn't believe that someone could produce high-quality art or writing in a short period of time. Mia thought Rodin's work was beautiful, precise, yet wild.

As long as a piece of art was enjoyed by others, nothing else mattered. Art had its own timetable. It didn't wait for man.

She went inside the Hotel Biron, the mansion where a majority of Rodin's work was housed. There were paintings, ceramics, prints, and more sculptures. Mia could have spent days in the little museum to look at everything. She hadn't even gone to the Louvre yet. When she did, she might spend an eternity there.

After a small French tour group moved on, Mia stepped in closer to look at *The Kiss*, Rodin's famous marble sculpture of a couple in a passionate embrace. They were characters from Dante's *Divine Comedy* who were later slain by the woman's husband, and the illicit lovers were condemned to spend eternity in hell.

Could a kiss have that much of an impact? Mia wondered. If she hadn't kissed Luc, would she still be as sad as she was now?

There were plenty of other men in the world, so why did she have to be stuck on one? One Frenchman on a scooter that she met on a rainy night in Montmartre. With striking blue eyes, a warm smile, and soft lips.

Now that she knew the truth, that Luc was in love with someone else, she should try to move on. Logically, she had every good reason to forget about him. If she could have her way, Luc would still be the leading man in her life.

Unfortunately, it wasn't up to her to decide. The man was in love with Beth. He had been for years. They were both French, rich, educated, and beautiful. They had even gone to the same school. It was obvious to everyone that they were well matched in every way.

And what had been there between her and Luc? Now that she thought about it, she was foolish to think there could've been something. Luc had only been nice to her because she was in the process of being mugged. They had shared a few laughs, but when he dropped her off, he didn't want to exchange contact information even as friends.

He had hired her because he needed a native English speaker. Since she was already a professional writer, he thought she could fit in well at his company. When he heard that she was looking for her sister, being the generous soul that he was, he naturally wanted to help her. Not because he was romantically interested in her. No. In fact, he probably felt sorry for her.

She sighed, looking longingly at the sculpture. This piece of marble was what romance looked like, frozen in time. She had shared a moment like this with Luc in the middle of a beautiful Parisian street. One of his hands had held her firmly on her back, the other tangled into her hair, his lips pressed firmly into hers. That had been the best kiss she'd ever had. Every nerve in her body had been tingling, every hair had stood on its end. Her brain couldn't function and the world had spun around her.

No other kiss had even come close. Sure, she'd had boyfriends, two serious relationships in total, but they had been light, fun relationships with little consideration for the future. Her career had been her main focus in her twenties. Luc was the first person she had felt a strong and unusual passion for. She could talk to him for hours and kiss those lips for eternity. However, his affections sailed toward Beth, and there was nothing she could do about it.

At least she still had Paris. The city of lights, the city of love, the most beautiful city in the world was all hers. She had the rest of the year to explore. She planned on poking around every beautiful street, every museum, every shop, every bridge on the Seine. There was still so much she hadn't done and all the people she had yet to meet. Mia was an optimist not by nature but by choice. There was plenty of good still to come. She had good friends, she had enough money to live on, a cozy apartment—there were plenty of blessings to count on.

As she wandered into a room of Rodin's paintings, she caught a glimpse of a young woman walking out of the room on the other side.

Mia's heart raced. The woman was as tall as she was but more slender. She had a similar Afro, and her skin was the same café au lait color as her own.

Was this the woman from the Fizz commercial—the sister Mia was looking for?

She quickened her pace, her boots pounding against the linoleum floor as she followed the young woman into a new section of the museum. Mia could only see the back of her head. She was wearing a navy-blue dress and black ballet flats. She was with a friend, a blond girl, and they were chatting before a sculpture of Camille Claudel.

Mia slowed down.

What was she supposed to ask her? "Excuse me, are you my long-lost sister?" Or "Pardon me, did you happen to be adopted at birth too?" What if the girl didn't even speak English?

The members of Les Slinks had called Luc back, including Luc's brother Mathieu. They didn't know anything about this woman. It was nice of Luc to have wanted to help, but with no new information on this woman, she was back at square one.

The two women continued into another room. Mia followed them, trying to get a view of the young woman's face. Her heart was beating like crazy. She'd been searching for a blood relative for so long, and now this potential sister was so close that it took her breath away.

Mia was only six feet behind them now, and she could hear them speaking in French. They were saying something about getting coffee, possibly in the café in the rose garden.

Mia took a deep breath. Panic seized her chest and words got lost along the way up her throat. She took another deep breath. It was now or never.

"Excusez-moi—"

The young woman turned around. Disappointment shot through Mia's soul.

It was not her. This woman bore no resemblance to Mia or the woman in the commercial. Her eyes were dark and rounded, her eyebrows thick and shaped like half moons, and her lips were wider, thinner.

"Nothing," Mia said, feeling stupid. "Never mind. Sorry."

She turned around and walked away, feeling her body shake. When she was at a sufficient distance from the two women, Mia sat down on a free bench. She put her head in her hands, suppressing a groan.

Of course it wasn't her. It would've been too easy.

But this was a reminder. She couldn't just depend on Luc or anyone else to find this person for her. She was on her own.

"You're in Paris for a reason," she told herself in a low voice. "You're searching for your sister. Don't get distracted."

CHAPTER EIGHTEEN

*B*eth gracefully pushed the knife into the lettuce and cut the leaves into infuriatingly small pieces. Luc watched her as she ate her kale salad with dainty bites then looked down at his own plate, which contained a hunk of duck. She never overloaded the fork, and she chewed inconspicuously, as if she was trying to pretend she wasn't chewing.

"What are you thinking about?" Beth asked him. "Your mind seems to be elsewhere."

Luc looked up at her again, this time meeting her ocean-colored eyes. Beth had pulled her blond hair back in a sophisticated chignon. She wore the most dazzling earrings, and her red lipstick must've been painted on, because the color never faded as she ate, nor did it leave noticeable lip prints on her wine glass.

She was, in a word, captivating.

All the men had turned to look at her when they entered the Michelin-starred restaurant together. He'd felt a surge of pride in that moment to know that he was being seen at the right place with the right woman, but those superficial types of recognition were never fulfilling in the long run.

By the time he sat down, he'd been ashamed of himself. What did he care what a bunch of strangers thought? Beth wasn't really his. Or rather, he didn't belong to Beth. They didn't belong to each other, and that became clear as the evening dragged on.

"I was just thinking about your campaign," he said. "It's a big step for us. There's so much to do."

He popped a piece of duck into his mouth and chewed. It tasted good, like all the other *confit de canard* he'd ever had, which was why he always ordered it. Yet he regretted ordering it; he should've tried something new.

"Let's not worry about that now." She reached across the table and put her hand over his. "Tonight is about us. We don't have to talk about business. With all that has been going on, we've been working nonstop. We can afford to unwind a little, right?" She raised her wine glass. "To us."

"To us," Luc obliged, clinking her glass and returning her smile.

Beth was wearing the most low-cut dress he'd ever seen her in. The amount of skin she showed would make a priest blush. It was poppy red, matching her lipstick, and the diamond necklace around her neck was perhaps meant to distract from her ample cleavage. Or draw attention to it.

Is she really trying this hard to impress me? Luc wondered.

Beth Montaigne, going above and beyond to please him for a change. It was almost unbelievable.

"Are you sure nothing's bothering you?" Beth was giving him another one of her strange looks.

"No, I don't think so. Although I do think the world is doomed and we're all going to die."

"Very funny." She took a tiny sip of her wine.

She had been the one who had picked the wine. Funny enough, it was the same one that Luc had picked for Mia the night they had kissed. Beth knew all about the wine, everything from the vineyard and the temperatures of the grapes to the fermentation times and the history of the owners.

When she swirled the wine in her glass, all Luc could think about was how he and Mia had joked about wine being basically grape juice. He had to suppress a laugh.

"You know, Luc, I'm very impressed with you." Beth leaned over her plate, speaking in a low voice as if she was trying to tell him a secret. "I don't think anyone else from our graduating class has been as successful as you."

"I don't think that's true. What about Claude, or Julien?"

"Oh, they didn't build a company from the ground up. Their success was handed to them. All they have to do is not fail, which isn't so hard when they already have competent people working beneath them, not to mention all that financial support from their families when the times got tough. I'm the same way. I don't deserve my success."

She looked up at him. This was his moment to interject and reassure her. Of course he did.

"That's not true, Beth. You graduated at the top of the class, and you seem to be making the right decisions so far with your company's new brand."

"Choosing your campaign, you mean?" She laughed lightly. "Sometimes I just wonder where I'd be if I were born middle class. Would I have more drive to succeed to prove myself?"

"I think so," Luc said. "You're not just a pretty face, you know. You're smart, too."

Beth fluttered her lashes. "You think I have a pretty face?"

"You know you do," he said. "It's a basic fact, such as the earth being round and the sky being blue. You don't need me to tell you that."

Beth sat back, satisfied. "Sure I do."

"Everybody thinks you're pretty," Luc said. "And you know it."

Beth laughed. "I didn't know that I knew."

"Don't pretend to be humble." Luc smiled. "I think you're clued in enough by all those men following you around campus and the marriage proposals that you probably get on a daily basis."

"Don't all girls get the same treatment?" Beth joked.

"I once saw a segment on TV about the science behind beauty. I bet your facial features would match the proportions of the ideal face."

Beth wrinkled her nose and laughed. "That sounds so cold and sterile. I was hoping for a comparison that was more poetic."

"I guess I'm not a poetic kind of guy. I definitely shouldn't be waxing poetic. I'll stick to advertising."

Luc took a sip of his own wine. He thought about how he'd compared Mia's beauty to the Rocky Mountains. The mountains, for Pete's sake. Was that poetic, or had that been stupid?

Beth laughed again.

Life is odd, Luc thought. The number-one thing on his life's wish list used to be to go on a romantic date with Beth, make her laugh, woo her, and make her fall in love with him.

While he enjoyed her company, it wasn't what he'd imagined it would be. Rather, this wasn't what he thought he would feel. He was living his fantasy, but he felt as if he was at dinner with one of his sisters. There was nothing wrong with Beth. She hadn't changed. She was still as lovely as always, polite, charming, graceful. But something was missing.

Beth wasn't Mia.

He had meant it when he said that Beth was beautiful. Any living human with working eyes could see that.

But Mia was a piece of art, priceless, moving, one of a kind. She made him feel things that were inexplicable, and she inspired him in ways he could never have predicted. She was the woman who came from nowhere whom he couldn't stop thinking about.

CHAPTER NINETEEN

"Sarah, you're a genius!"

Mia jumped out of her seat and gave Sarah a big hug, causing a few of the employees who were back from lunch to turn and give them weird looks.

"I wouldn't go that far." Sarah grinned proudly nonetheless. "I'm on a computer all day. I know my way around one."

"What's going on?" Amélie came by.

"You know how I'm looking for someone who could be my sister?"

"Why? Did you find her?" Amélie asked excitedly.

"Not yet, but Sarah created a Facebook page for me. Here."

Mia showed her what Sarah had taken only her lunch break to put together. Sarah had put up a screen shot of the woman from the Fizz commercial next to a photo of Mia. Sarah also linked to the Fizz commercial on LUX's company website.

"*Doppelgängers or Sisters?*" Amélie read out loud. "*Mia Golden was watching YouTube when a Fizz commercial popped up. In the background, there was an extra who resembled her. Adopted at birth, Mia has never known her birth parents, but she believes that there is a high chance that she is related to the woman pictured. If you have any leads on who this woman is, please contact Sarah Christie.* Wow, the search is on."

"It's only been live for a few minutes," Sarah said. "Fingers crossed that this will go viral and we'll find her in no time."

"What about your parents, Mia?" Amélie asked. "What if they saw this page?"

"Well, last weekend, I decided to be honest with them. We Skyped, and I finally told them that my decision to move to Paris wasn't all about taking a yearlong break from journalism or trying to learn French."

"Were they hurt?"

"Yes, but mainly because I didn't tell them sooner. I thought they would be hurt that I wanted to find a blood relative, but I should've given them more credit. I made them watch the Fizz commercial, and they agreed that this woman looks just like me. My mom even said there's a chance that we could be twins. Fraternal twins at least. They really do understand why I would want to find this woman. Everybody wants to find a piece of themselves in someone else."

"I always thought my little brother was a pain in the butt growing up," Sarah said. "But after hearing Mia's story, I appreciate him more. There's something to be said about relating to someone who shares your blood."

Amélie nodded. "You have my full support. This girl might be French, and I can spread the post to my French network. Hey, why don't I help you translate the page?"

"That would be fantastic," Mia said. "You know, just this morning I was thinking just how impossible it was to find this girl. All the adoption agencies in this city simply will not help me whatsoever. I understand their point of view, but I was just defeated. I don't know why I didn't think of this before. Use the power of the Internet, of course."

"The world is more connected than ever," Sarah said. "If the Internet doesn't find our girl at this point, nothing will."

"I think you'll find her," Amélie agreed. "Facebook campaigns are good with these types of things. I remember a story from two years ago. This one American guy had traveled to Australia during the holidays. He met and kissed a local girl on New Year's Eve, but she didn't give him her contacts. All he had was her first name and a picture of them together on his phone. I don't know why she did that. Maybe she was trying to be mysterious or wasn't serious about him. When he went back to America, he couldn't stop thinking about her, and he made a similar page, asking people to help him find her. He got a lot of leads."

"What happened in the end?" Mia asked.

"I think he did find her. Unfortunately she was in a relationship, and she had to delete her Facebook and other social media accounts because so many people were messaging her to the point of harassment."

"Oh." Mia looked at the computer again, having second thoughts this time. "She probably didn't want to be found to begin with. What if this woman doesn't want to be found either, even if it turns out that she is my sister?"

"Well," Sarah said slowly, "the point is that the guy tried."

"Right," Amélie agreed. "If he didn't try to find her, he might've lived with the regret of letting go of someone that he thought was the love of his life. He would've idealized her and the night they shared for years. It was better that he found her and got a dose of reality. She wasn't interested and she had moved on. It's painful, but at least that allowed him to move on."

"What about this woman?" Mia asked. "What if she gets mad that her picture is all over the Internet?"

"I'm sure she has pictures of herself on the Internet already," Amélie said. "If she ever complains, we can always take it down. She's already in a Youtube video. At least you'd know her stance on this whole thing if you find her."

"So stick with it," Sarah encouraged. "Don't worry. Even if you didn't find your sister, you found us. You have to make your family, especially when you move to a new country by yourself."

Mia smiled. "Thanks, girls."

"Send me the link to the page, Sarah," Amélie said. "I'll start translating it now."

"Are you sure it's okay to work on it during company time?" Mia asked. "More people will be coming back from lunch soon. I don't want you to get in trouble. Especially with Brigette and Lina."

"It'll be fine," Amélie said. "They won't notice. They'll be too busy gossiping about Luc and his date with the Montaigne heiress to care what I'm doing."

Mia's heart fell. Her expression must've fallen as well, but Amélie and Sarah were too distracted by the Facebook page to notice.

"They went on a date?" Mia tried to ask casually.

"Dinner at this snooty restaurant," Amélie said. "Chez Antoine. Somebody here saw them. Alec in accounting."

"Chez Antoine?" Sarah exclaimed. "I heard about that place. It's impossible to get in! I heard that there's like a three-month waiting list to eat there."

"That's funny, because Alec wasn't in the restaurant. It wasn't as if he got in either. He saw the two of them walking out of the restaurant."

"Were they all lovey-dovey?" Sarah asked. "Maybe it was just a business dinner."

"I doubt it," Amélie said. "Everybody here knows that Luc's been in love with Beth for a long time. The dinner was not business related. Alec said that Beth was wearing the most seductive red dress. You don't dress that way for a business dinner."

Mia gulped. She could imagine. Beth had a gorgeous body. There was no reason Luc would resist dating someone like her.

"So are they an item now?" Mia asked. "Luc and Beth?"

"Probably," Amélie said. "She was even here at the office earlier that day. I guess they'll be spending a lot of time together, since they're working on the campaign and everything."

Mia shouldn't care about who Luc dated, but it hurt. She hadn't realized it would hurt this much.

"Beth is really beautiful, isn't she?" she said.

CHAPTER TWENTY

*I*f only Luc's personal life was going as well as his professional life. LUX had just won a major campaign over two other top French ad agencies for the nation's leading dish soap, and things were looking good for all their other pitches. The Mademoiselle Montaigne commercial was going to be shot at the end of the week, and Didier and the Montaigne company had already arranged for the print ads to run in numerous fashion and luxury lifestyle magazines.

Everybody was excitedly anticipating the public response to the lingerie ads. A few of his employees had suggested that it could turn into an iconic campaign. Didier was even optimistic about their chances of being nominated for the best ad agency in Paris that year. Luc didn't want to get his hopes up, but he had a good feeling about this one.

There was a lot going on at LUX, but Luc made a habit of starting his mornings off alone in his office in a quiet moment of reflective peace. He sipped his espresso, looking out the window at the blue dome rooftop of the building across the street and the blue sky above.

He tried not to think about Mia.

Her words still stung him.

"Let's *just forget it ever happened*," she had said.

Maybe in America, a kiss didn't mean much. He'd been surprised during his semester in Utah, where his American classmates would kiss different girls at campus parties on the same weekend. "Hooking up" was what they called it.

In France, if you kissed somebody, you were in a relationship. It must've been a cultural difference. Perhaps that was why a kiss meant so little to Mia, why she thought a kiss didn't mean a lot to him, or both.

He wondered whether she was rejecting *him* or the idea of a workplace relationship. Perhaps she was embarrassed. After all, he was her boss, not the other way around. Maybe she didn't want to jeopardize her job or was embarrassed that she had been drunk when it happened.

No matter how he tried to justify her words, they still hurt. Did she really mean them, or was she trying to protect herself somehow? Usually she was so open with her feelings that he thought he could read her, but her expression had been shut down that day, completely blank. She couldn't meet his eyes, and her voice had been cold and lifeless.

He closed his eyes. The same scene flashed back to him. Mia sitting in front of his desk. He had been on the verge of asking her out when she tried to make light of their kiss.

His eyes opened in realization: she didn't know how he felt about her. He had never told her. If she knew how much he was interested in her, perhaps she would reconsider.

It was a tricky line to cross, however. If she simply didn't like him, he didn't want to come on too strong, especially since he was her superior.

He picked up the phone to speak to his secretary.

"Can you ask Mia to come into my office, please?"

After he hung up, he leaned back in his chair and tried to relax. He was a picture of professional calm, but on the inside, his heart was beating like crazy. His palms were sweating and the room was getting warmer by the second.

What was he, thirteen again? At that age, he'd been so shy around girls. His brothers would tease him, and Luc had to force himself to get out of his shell.

Slowly, throughout his teen years, he had gotten better and better at talking to girls. It turned out that the girls he liked weren't so scary after all. They usually responded favorably or were nice about it if they weren't interested. It helped that he had two sisters and a doting mother, so he knew how to treat a girl.

His experiences had taught him that fear was just an illusion. Now getting over his fears was second nature. Whatever he wanted, he went out and got it, which had contributed to his successes in life so far. He rarely let his fears get the best of him.

Almost.

So he had dragged his feet when it came to Beth. If only he hadn't been so intimidated by her, he would've had the guts to properly ask her out. That way, he would've known sooner rather than later that they didn't click romantically and that they were better off as friends. He wouldn't have wasted so much time chasing after someone just because everyone else wanted her.

Now he wasn't going to do the same with Mia. She would only be in Paris for a year. Two months were already up, and they had ten months left. There was no way he would let her slip through his fingers. Time could pass so quickly. There was no way he wasn't going to try to see if he was right, that there was really something between them.

Mia's knock startled him. She poked her head in before she entered.

"Am I disturbing you?"

"No, not at all." Luc sat up. "Come on in."

"I heard you wanted to see me. Is it about the Damour campaign?"

Her tone was brisk and businesslike. In response, he found himself tapping his fingers on the desk from the tension. Luc had been hoping for more of the easygoing friendliness they used to share. What had changed?

He had forgotten about the Damour campaign, but it was something they were supposed to start on.

"Right, the Damour campaign. Have you ever visited their patisseries?"

Mia sat down in her usual spot. She was looking everywhere but at him.

"No, not yet, but I heard they have the best macarons in the city."

"They do," Luc said. "Their green tea macarons are my favorite."

Mia only nodded. She seemed distant.

Luc cleared his throat. Mia's bright eyes fluttered and grazed over his before her lashes lowered. She looked down at her hands.

"They want to run a series of ads for the store's twentieth anniversary," Luc said. "They have patisseries around the world, and they want to run the ads in a lot of luxury publications, from fashion to travel to gourmet food magazines and websites. It'll be in French and English."

"Too bad they don't have a store in Seattle," Mia said.

Luc smiled. At least she was starting to look more comfortable in his presence.

"The ads need to be classy but not stuffy. You're good with tasteful humor. Think you can take a crack at it?"

He found the Damour file on his desk and passed it to her.

"Sure." Mia opened the file to Damour's company information. "Their desserts look beautiful. I'm sure they'll inspire me to come up with something halfway decent."

"Actually," Luc said slowly, "they have a great *salon de thé* in the 16th. We can eat lunch there together. That is, if you're free. It's on the company."

"Oh." Mia seemed to be considering it. "You mean, today?"

"Yes. We'll take the company car there, and actually, I wanted to speak to you about something."

"I would." She bit her lip. "But I promised Sarah, Amélie, and a couple of other girls that I'd go to lunch with them. Sarah really helped me out with something and I wanted to treat her."

Luc was impressed that the other employees had warmed up to Mia. He had known some of the French staff would like Mia as soon as they got to know her.

"Is it because of the website?" Luc asked. "The Facebook page? I heard the employees talking about it, and later Sarah sent me the link. Did anybody contact you so far?"

"Only messages of support." Mia's soft lips eased into a smile. "Nothing really to go on yet, but fingers crossed."

"About that. My brother came home from touring yesterday, finally. I went over to his place, and we had a long chat about the situation. As I've mentioned, he doesn't recognize the girl at all, but we're brainstorming about other ways we can get a hold of her."

"That's okay, Luc. You've done more than you needed to. It's really okay. I have a good feeling about this Facebook thing."

Luc nodded. "So maybe we can do lunch another time then. Tomorrow?"

"You really don't have to take time out of your busy schedule. I know you usually like to have a quick lunch at your desk. I think I'll just visit all their patisseries in the city during the weekend. That way, I'll be able to observe, eat, and write at the same time."

"Oh, sure. Whatever you feel would work best for you." Luc tried not to sound disappointed.

"You said you wanted to talk to me about something?"

"Yes." Luc had second thoughts about professing his feelings for her in the office.

However, he was supposed to seize the moment, right? Not let her slip between his fingers?

But what was he supposed to say? He couldn't just ask her out on a date given how uncomfortable she was when faced with the prospect of going to lunch with him.

Then the solution hit him, and he brightened up.

After his evening out with Beth, she'd invited him to Mademoiselle Montaigne's store-opening party. He was allowed to invite all the friends and employees of his choosing. If Mia came, it would be the perfect place and time to tell her how he felt. It wasn't exactly a social event, and it wasn't exactly work related.

"Mia, you know where the new Mademoiselle Montaigne store will be, right? Three doors down from the Madame Montaigne flagship store on at the Rue Saint-Honoré."

Mia nodded. "I've visited Madame Montaigne once."

"Well, Mademoiselle Montaigne is having a store opening next Saturday night. I was wondering if you'd like to go."

Mia blinked at him. Luc was afraid she was about to say no.

"Some of the other employees will be going too," he added quickly. "Didier, of course."

"Really?" Mia was still thinking. "Sarah and Amélie as well?"

"Yes. You can even bring a few friends if you'd like."

"Really? I have a couple of friends from French class who would enjoy coming to something like this. Amanda especially. She loves the Montaigne line."

Luc beamed at her. Having her say yes to the party meant a lot to him.

"Then it's settled. It begins at eight p.m., and I'll tell Beth to put you plus two guests on the list. The dress code is formal." He cleared his throat. "Would you like a ride?"

"Oh, that's not necessary," Mia said. "Who knows when the girls and I will be ready. We'll find our own way, don't worry."

Luc had meant that he wanted to pick up Mia only. They were speaking the same language, English, but their communication was cross-wired. Somehow he'd imagined picking Mia up on his Vespa, like he had on the first night they met. But he couldn't blame Mia. He hadn't exactly made it clear that he wanted to take her to the party as his date.

"How are French classes going anyway?" Luc asked.

"*Bien*. I still have a long way to go." She paused. "See? I don't even know how to say that in French yet."

CHAPTER TWENTY-ONE

"*I* don't want to go to work every day knowing that Luc is pining for Beth," Mia blurted out. "I think I'm going to quit."

Amanda and Kiko were at her apartment, already in elegant dresses for the Montaigne party.

Kiko, who had always been the more sensible one, shook her head. "Don't quit. I thought you liked your job."

"I do," Mia said. "I'm liking my coworkers more and more, and the work is fun. Different from journalism, but it's been a fantastic experience."

"Not to mention all the benefits and the free French classes," Kiko said. "You can't throw it all away."

Amanda took a sip of her wine. "I understand how you feel, Mia. I used to work in corporate before I decided that lifestyle wasn't for me. Then I trained to be a yoga teacher and ran away to Paris. Anyway, back then, I was in a serious relationship with a guy in my office named Michael. We went out for almost a year. He looked just like Clint Eastwood, back when he was young and hot. I was hopelessly, head-over-heels in love with the guy. Michael dumped me and started seeing one of my coworkers. Can you imagine? I tried to be strong at first, but I couldn't help feeling bitter and angry whenever I saw them together. In the end, I quit. I didn't like working in an office anyway, but even if I did, I think I would've tried to find another job. It wasn't worth it."

Mia sat down on the couch beside Amanda and put an arm around her. "I didn't know that. Heartbreaks suck." She shook her head. "It's silly because at least you went out with the guy for a year. Nothing even happened between Luc and me. I shouldn't be this devastated."

"You kissed," Kiko reminded her. "Remember?"

"It was a drunken kiss. It doesn't count. It's just been really awkward between us at the office lately ever since that happened. I don't even know how to act like myself around him anymore. It's like I turned into a robot."

"I have to say," Amanda said, "I still can't get over how you two met. He saves you from getting mugged in the middle of the night in Montmartre, and then you meet him again the next morning in his office? That's some cosmic stuff right there. It was as if the universe was conspiring to get you guys together."

Amanda sighed romantically. Mia wished she could believe it, too, dive headfirst into the highs of love, but she had to be a realist.

"Luc doesn't belong to me," she said. "He belongs to Beth."

"But Mia," Amanda protested. "Does Luc even know how you feel? Do you even know how he feels? He invited you to this party. That means something, doesn't it?"

"He invited me because I came up with the Montaigne campaign. Besides, you haven't met Beth. You will tonight. Then you'll see why she's perfect for Luc."

"Fine," Kiko said. "We'll see about that. I'm pretty good at sensing people's romantic chemistry. If I don't think Luc and Beth will make a good couple, you have to tell him how you feel."

"But—"

Amanda turned to Mia and looked her in the eye. "I get it, Mia, I do. Love is scary. But if you think about it, you have nothing to lose. You said it yourself. You're not going to be working in advertising forever anyway. What's a little humiliation? If there's even a chance that he'd feel the same, it's worth taking that chance."

Mia knew Amanda was right. Admitting her feelings to Luc would be the brave thing to do. Mia had always thought of herself as brave, but in this circumstance, she had turned into a coward.

She shook her head. "I can't."

"You're afraid of love, Mia. But I can't tell if you're afraid of being hurt or afraid of getting what you want."

"I want love," Mia said without much conviction. She sighed. "Maybe I'm not ready. Maybe I'm afraid to be disappointed. Look at the situation with my doppelgänger. I'm trying to be patient, but it's something I can't control. There's a chance I may never find her and that she may not even exist. I don't think I can take another major disappointment right now."

"Despite your fears, you're here in Paris," Amanda said. "You've packed up your life in Seattle and moved all the way here because you wanted to take a chance. You're braver than you think."

Kiko nodded. "She's right. You came to Paris by yourself, knowing no one at all. Everybody in the office hated you at first, but you maintained a positive attitude, won a major campaign, and now you have plenty of friends at work."

"You're functioning in a country where you barely speak the language," Amanda added.

"The French speak pretty good English," Mia said. "I was surprised."

"You've put yourself out there on the Internet to find your sister," Kiko continued. "What's one more thing? All you have to do is tell Luc the truth. A little rejection never killed anybody."

Mia laughed. "I'm not sure about that."

"You know what I mean. It's not a life-or-death situation. Even if he does reject you, it's his loss. You have so much to offer to a man."

"Also," Amanda chipped in, "you shouldn't be comparing yourself to this Beth woman. I don't care how gorgeous she is. Everyone has something different to offer."

"Thanks. You're right. I don't know why we women have to do that. It's not healthy. I see Beth, and I think she has it all, but really, I don't know anything about her."

"I don't think any woman really has it all together," Kiko said. "But we sure pretend. Someone else could be looking at you and thinking that *you* have everything."

"True," Amanda said. "You never know how you may seem to others. Appearances are just illusions."

Mia stood up and looked appreciatively at her two strong and inspiring new friends. Amanda was in a bright-orange floor-length gown, with lipstick to match. She looked fun, fresh, and sophisticated at the same time. Kiko was in a classy plum strapless satin dress and wore a diamond necklace.

"If appearances are illusions, should I be telling you that you both look gorgeous?" Mia said. "Or did I tell you that already?"

"Numerous times." Amanda smiled.

"I'm going to go change. I think we're already late."

"Don't worry about it," Amanda said. "Being fashionably late is so common around here."

Mia went into the bathroom, where her own dress was hung behind the door. She'd better hurry, because she didn't want to be disrespectful and be too late. The party had already started. It was a work-related event, after all.

When Luc had first invited her to the party, she had been hesitant. She didn't want to see for herself whether Luc and Beth were an item. If she were to see them dancing and canoodling, she didn't know how she would bear it.

But the more she thought about it, going to the party would be a good idea. If she wanted to be fearless, she had to face the truth. If Luc and Beth were in love, it would be good to know before she declared her feelings to Luc.

Mia fixed her wild hair back with a faux diamond headband. Amanda helped her with the eye shadow, since she was a lot better at applying makeup than Mia was. After that, she slipped into her new dress.

She'd found the dress in the gorgeous Galeries Lafayette department store when she went shopping with Amélie and Sarah after work earlier that week. The dress cost almost as much as her rent, but her friends had convinced her to try it on. The emerald-green color brought out the green in her eyes and complemented her skin tone, and the silk fabric hung so well over her body that it felt like a second skin.

When she had looked at price tag, she'd gulped.

"It's not that expensive," Amélie had argued. "This is a party of a lifetime. Celebrities and the Parisian elite will be there."

"When you look good, you feel good," Sarah had added.

Mia didn't like the fact that how she felt about herself was dependent on how she looked, but she remembered feeling out of place in Beth's office wearing her discount clothing. She was a woman, after all, and she did want to feel pretty. This dress was everything she wanted. Emerald green was her color, the cut was modest and flattering, and she felt comfortable in it. She had to have it.

"*C'est belle.*" Kiko's jaw dropped when Mia came out.

Amanda stood up. "Wow. I thought the dress looked just okay on the hanger, but on you—"

Mia smiled. In truth, she didn't think she looked half bad. It was a simple dress, but the best things in life were simple.

"I never knew you had such great curves," Amanda added. "I'm so jealous. Even if Luc is into this Beth chick, all the guys at the party will be lining up to talk to you. But I kind of doubt Luc will want to take his eyes off you."

"You don't even need any jewelry," Kiko said. "You're a natural beauty. The headband gives you enough sparkle."

"Luc will be lost in a sea of emerald," Amanda said coyly.

Mia looked at herself in the mirror. She did think she looked beautiful. And even though she tried not to feel that way, she couldn't help getting excited knowing that Luc would see her soon.

CHAPTER TWENTY-TWO

*M*oney. Luc could see it, taste it, and almost smell it as soon as he entered the Montaigne party. It reminded him of his time at university with Beth, when he was constantly surrounded by peers with inheritances, stocks, bonds, and vacation houses galore.

A gigantic silver chandelier hung over him like an all-seeing eye, reflecting gold and silver specks. Gentlemen in tuxedos held flutes of champagne as they chatted up ladies wearing four-figure gowns. Five figures wouldn't surprise him, either. And some of the jewels must've been in the six-figure range.

Luc had come in with Didier and Charlotte, Didier's wife. Nondescript men in white tuxedos took their coats. Fancy, tiny hors d'oeuvres on silver trays floated in and out of their periphery, as did the champagne. The champagne tasted good, and so did the grilled scallops wrapped in prosciutto, but Luc had gone to too many of these parties to be impressed anymore.

"The ads look great," Didier commented.

Gigi Tom's photograph in which she was in a black lace lingerie set, wearing a pink holster and a matching gun, was the framed centerpiece of the room. Other ads from the campaign featuring Gigi portraying film noir femme fatales lined the walls as well.

"You've outdone yourselves this time, boys," Charlotte said. "It's quite cheeky."

"The commercial is coming along too," Luc said. "They're putting the final editing touches on it, and it should be on TV and on the Internet next week."

Didier and Charlotte were accosted by some friends, and they quickly engaged in conversation. Luc spent some time chatting with them then politely excused himself.

He looked around for the only person he was looking forward to seeing that night. Would she even come? He looked at his watch. It was almost nine thirty.

"Luc!" a cheerful voice called out to him.

He spun around and found himself inches away from Beth Montaigne.

"*Bonsoir*, Beth." He greeted her the usual way, with kisses on both cheeks.

Her last kiss lingered, and he could smell her perfume. She was in a shimmery gold dress, which gave her the illusion of being dipped in liquid gold. He thought she looked like a statue or a trophy.

As usual, a group of men was swarming around her, some discreetly and others not so discreetly.

"Have you met Marcus, Benjamin, and Renard?"

"No." Beth introduced him to what he assumed were her potential suitors, although it soon became clear that Marcus was gay.

"Marcus designed my dress," Beth said.

"It's beautiful," Luc said. "You look great, as usual."

"It's custom made just for her," said Marcus. "Her body's every designer's dream. It's perfect."

"Oh, stop." Beth laughed. "Nobody's perfect."

Luc smiled politely.

She glanced back at Luc and grabbed his arm. "Come on, let's dance."

Benjamin and Renard, as well as a few other men lingering around, looked disappointed as Beth dragged Luc off to the dance floor.

A jazz band was playing a slow number, and Beth wrapped her arms around his neck.

"It's a great party," Luc said.

It was strange to have Beth pressed so close to him. It was obvious that many men would want to be in his position right now, but he still found himself wanting to be in the arms of someone else.

"I've gotten great feedback on the campaign so far," Beth said. "Our website and social media numbers are off the charts. I shouldn't have doubted you and your team for a moment."

Luc smiled. "Actually, it's okay to. Nothing's ever a sure thing. Not in advertising, not in life." And not in love, he silently added. "But you have to take a chance once in a while."

"I find that we French are so afraid to fail," Beth said. "Not like the Americans. That's why their country is chaotic, but I have to admit, that's probably why they're so innovative as well. I'll never tell that to an American, though."

Beth's laugh tinkled in his ear.

Money. The word came to Luc again. That was how Nick Carraway described Daisy's laugh in *The Great Gatsby*.

Beth had been his Daisy all along. He'd spent years trying to be the man he thought she wanted him to be.

Now that Luc had the money and the respect, Beth had decided to give him a chance.

But Luc wasn't going to make the same mistake that Gatsby had. As they danced, her perfume engulfing him, he realized that Beth had been a dream, and Luc had woken up a long time ago and realized that reality was better.

Reality came in the form of a woman who looked just like America. Now just where was she already?

"Oh look," Beth said. "Gigi Tom came. And she brought her latest rock-star boyfriend." She wrinkled her nose. "I wish she hadn't. He's supposed to have this severe cocaine problem. I hope he doesn't cause a scene tonight."

Luc turned and saw the cool supermodel walking in. He'd been working with her all week. The rock-star boyfriend in question, Sam Smitheron, from the Deadly Vines, a band his brother's band had toured with, was cracking jokes with the waiters. The cocaine problem was probably true, but Luc had met the dark-haired Englishman a couple of times. Sam was nice if Beth would only get to know him. He could see why models like Gigi liked him. He was funny, sensitive, and poetic and one of the best songwriters of his generation. One of Mathieu's bandmates had had a cocaine problem before he got help, and Luc had learned not to judge people so harshly based on their weaknesses. If Sam really did have a cocaine problem, he hoped he would get help soon.

As he watched the famous couple, his gaze fell behind them to the most beautiful woman in the room.

She wore a simple emerald dress, and her wild hair was untamed even by a headband. Everything about her shone as if she were lit up from within. Her smile brightened up the party, which had been stuffy so far.

Mia was looking around in awe, smiling and talking to her friends excitedly. Luc smiled. He knew she would enjoy the party. He had found these kinds of events fun too when he first started coming to them, when he'd been more impressed by grandeur.

Mia was now chatting with Gigi Tom. He wouldn't be surprised if the two of them became BFFs by the end of the week. Mia could make friends with anyone. Even Lina, one of his most difficult employees at LUX, who rarely liked anyone, was starting to thaw around Mia.

"Luc." It was Beth, looking at him with concern. "Did you see someone you recognize?"

"Yes," he said. "A peer." The song was over. He extracted himself from her embrace. "I'm going to say hi, if you'll excuse me."

"Of course." Beth's voice was flat. She pulled away.

Luc turned back in Mia's direction. It was as if she was a magnet pulling him to her.

He'd just seen her at the office yesterday, but tonight was different. Tonight he was going to tell her that he loved her.

CHAPTER TWENTY-THREE

*W*hen Luc eased his hand away from Beth's arm, she fought the urge to hold onto him. As Beth watched him walk away from her, she kept a smile on her face. She glanced around, wondering if anyone had witnessed that small moment of rejection. No man had ever done that to her before.

She had always thought that Luc liked her. She used to catch him staring at her with his puppyish blue eyes in lecture halls when they were both studying at the same university. He was one of those guys who was always hovering around her, waiting for an opening to talk to her. He looked at her like she was a goddess.

Throughout the years, he had been a regular at her social circle's gatherings. Whenever she threw a party, he always showed up alone, holding a thoughtful present for her. He gave her the kind of attention that a girl could get used to.

She had to admit that she had taken it for granted. They both dated others casually, and Beth had put Luc in the friend category. It wasn't that she wasn't interested, but with so many options, how was she supposed to decide?

As she watched him move between guests, dodging cater waiters and even the gorgeous supermodel, Gigi Tom, Beth felt her heart drop to her gut. She had a feeling who Luc was walking toward.

Mia Golden was here at the party. She was a LUX employee who'd come up with the campaign idea for her Mademoiselle Montaigne line. Mia was certainly not as pretty as Beth was, she knew that, but Mia had something. Her hair was too curly and a bit wild, but it certainly commanded attention. She didn't have the ideal model's body—her hips were wide, out of proportion to her smaller chest—but she had lovely skin. From what Beth remembered of her at the pitch meeting, Mia also had beautiful eyes, hazel-green eyes that flashed brightly when she was making a passionate speech.

And Mia's smile now, as she responded to Luc, was wide, as dazzling as the chandelier over her head.

Beth sighed.

Her friend Marcus sensed her distress. He took her hands, and they waltzed on the dance floor.

"Something troubling you, Beth darling?" Marcus asked.

"Why?" Beth asked. "Do I not look okay?"

"You look as beautiful as always, which I'm sure you're tired of hearing. But you do look a bit pale."

Marcus Savin was one of her closest friends. He could see right through her.

"I–"

How was she supposed to explain it? For as long as she could remember, she had been used to being the center of attention whenever she walked into a room. She had always taken that attention for granted, figuring that she could take her time, picking and choosing whoever she wanted when she wanted. She had waited too long; she'd given Luc enough space for him to fall in love with someone else.

"I need a drink," Beth said. "And the dancing is making me dizzy."

They went to the edge of the dance floor, where Marcus grabbed a glass of white wine off a waiter's tray and gave it to Beth. "Come on. Let's go sit down."

She sat down on a black leather couch by the wall and downed half the glass.

"Are you feeling all right, Beth? Is it this flu going around? One of my friends is sick in bed. It's incredibly nasty."

Beth smiled sadly. "I wish it were medical, Marcus."

"Oh, quit being so dramatic. Spill it."

She took a deep breath and looked back at Luc and Mia. They were walking off somewhere together, perhaps out to the back of the store, which led to a small garden.

"Have you ever had the feeling that you made a huge mistake in life? That you missed a major boat that came your way, and now it's sailing away?"

Marcus shook his head. "Whatever happened was meant to happen. I never have regrets, none whatsoever."

"Well, I do."

Marcus looked up in the direction Beth was looking. "This isn't about a boy, is it? That boy?"

She slowly nodded.

"You're kidding. Beth Montaigne? Your biggest problem when it comes to men is who to beat away with a stick on any given day."

Beth let out a low laugh. She blinked as if she was having trouble focusing her eyes. "What good is it if the only person you realize you wanted doesn't want you anymore?"

"Who wouldn't want you? You're Beth Montaigne, for Chrissake."

"Luc Deneuve. You just met him. He just left."

"Luc, I must admit, is quite delicious. He must be gay if he doesn't want you. You don't mind if I take a stab, do you?"

Beth hit Marcus playfully on the arm.

"He's in love with someone else now." She put a delicate hand on her head. It was throbbing now. The wine wasn't helping. "I waited too long, and now it's too late."

"What do you mean you waited too long?"

"I always thought Luc was cute and smart, but there was never a shortage of guys around me. Plus, I was so busy with work and building my career that I didn't give him the time of day. I can't believe it took me so long to see how special Luc is. Not only is he handsome and smart, he's caring and generous. I know a lot of men who are successful and good looking, but how many are also thoughtful and kindhearted? And now his heart belongs to someone else."

"Oh, Beth," Marcus said, softening up. "You're really in love with him? Are you sure it's too late? Are you sure he's in love with someone else?"

"He is. I've noticed the shift in him ever since he met Mia. She's American, and she works for Luc."

"I'm sure whoever she is, she's no match for you."

"No, Marcus, I really don't think I'm in the running anymore."

"You're as beautiful as a top model, you're rich, you're educated, you have men lined up for miles. Who is this Mia girl and what does she have on you?"

Beth sighed. "She's actually rather talented. She was the one who came up with the idea for the 'Protect Your Valuables' campaign. She's beautiful in an exotic way. I have to admit, if I didn't resent her right now, I'd like her."

"So what? There are plenty of talented and beautiful girls in the city. Didn't you say that

Luc was in love with you for years? What would change now? Just because he's talking to her doesn't mean he's in love with her."

"No." Beth shook her head. "You haven't heard how they met."

She told Marcus the story Luc had told her about how Luc had met Mia randomly in the middle of the night in Montmartre. Then how Mia had stumbled into his office the next morning, not knowing that he was interviewing copywriters. How he'd hired her, just like that. Life's strange little coincidences.

"They're fated to be together," Beth said. "I think he's been enamored with her from day one. I've been trying to get his attention these past few weeks. We even went out for dinner, and I was the one who asked him. I've never asked a man out in my life. The whole time he seemed distracted and disinterested, and now I know why. You should've seen the way his face lit up when he saw Mia come in just now. That was how he used to look at me, and he doesn't anymore."

"Beth, I'm sorry."

Marcus stood up and put out his hand. She took it, standing up too.

"Life is full of curveballs, isn't it, Marcus?"

"Come on, let's dance it off." Marcus dragged her back onto the dance floor. The jazz band was playing a slow song again. "You're not used to being disappointed, are you? This must be especially hard for you."

"I guess this is what it feels like. Heartbreak."

"It's a mild form of heartbreak. You'll get over it. Sweetie, you don't even know the meaning of heartbreak yet. I bet you do worse to boys on a daily basis."

Beth put her head on his shoulder. "I guess I'll just categorize this as one of my life's big regrets so far."

"Oh, don't be so melodramatic. I don't feel sorry for you one bit. Do you see all these single men around here, dying to get a dance with you?"

Beth laughed. "They're also here for the Montaigne lingerie show later in the evening. You know, all the half-naked women you're not interested in."

"Give me a break. At least I'm interested in the lingerie."

Beth laughed again. "Marcus, you're so funny. Why can't you be straight? You'd be the perfect man for me."

CHAPTER TWENTY-FOUR

*J*f there ever had been a moment in time when Mia had the chance to feel like a princess, it was at the Montaigne party. The decor, the food, the music—it was as if she'd stumbled onto the set of a movie. The decadence was unreal, and the people were beautiful. Everybody was wearing the most beautiful clothes and jewels, and it was as if she was attending a palace ball.

It also helped that shots of the Montaigne ad campaign lined the walls. A surge of pride rose in her chest at knowing that she was responsible for the idea. The girls in the ads looked beautiful and strong. In the main campaign photo, Gigi Tom looked back at the viewer as if challenging them to defy her.

"If this is supposed to be a lingerie shop," Amanda remarked, "the Victoria's Secrets back home might as well be Walmarts."

"Most of the guests here are millionaires," Amélie said. "They probably don't even know what a Walmart is."

"Of course not," Kiko said. "They come from families who haven't mowed their own lawns for over three hundred years."

"Fancy schmancy." Sarah grinned. "I heard there's going to be a lingerie show later."

"Ohh, free champagne," Kiko gushed.

"Don't mind if I do." Amanda plucked one from a waiter's tray.

The others did the same.

"Cheers." Amélie raised her glass.

Mia grinned. So she didn't have a prince, but who said you needed a prince to feel like a princess? Four of her girlfriends were here with her, and she was going to try her best to have an amazing time at the party.

As they all drank up, Kiko's eyes widened.

"Look, isn't that Gigi Tom?"

Mia and the others tried to look at the blond supermodel discreetly. Gigi was with her on-and-off-again musician boyfriend.

Mia had read about them online. Not that she was proud to be reading celebrity gossip, but when she'd had to keep up with the news as a journalist, she would read the entertainment sections from time to time as a break from all the serious and depressing world news.

Gigi was in a shimmery flapper-inspired silver dress, and her boyfriend still had his rocker edge in a tux, given his overgrown hair and dark under-eye circles. He looked as if he was used to partying every night of the week.

"Let's go say hi to her," Mia said.

"Who?" Amélie asked.

"Gigi, of course."

"What? You can't—"

Mia was already in front of the supermodel, introducing herself with a big smile. Life was too short to be intimidated by anyone. Gigi turned out to be quite friendly and chatty, and Mia's friends shyly gathered around her, asking her questions about the modeling industry. Sam, the rocker boyfriend, was also quite nice, and funny too, cracking a joke a minute.

As Gigi's boyfriend was telling a story about how they met, Amanda nudged Mia.

"Hey, isn't that your hot boss coming this way?"

Mia looked up like a deer in headlights. She had known she was going to see Luc around sooner or later, but she had expected to have some time to prepare herself. He was only ten feet away and coming closer.

"Mia?" Luc said, smiling widely and meeting her eyes. "You look beautiful."

"Thanks." Mia could feel herself blushing. "Good evening, Luc."

Luc didn't look half bad himself. He looked every inch the dashing young prince. She wondered where Beth was, the real princess of the party.

"Mia," Amanda said, "this is your boss? The man in the cape and tights who saved you from that mugging in Montmartre?"

Luc laughed and stuck out a hand for Amanda to shake.

Mia introduced them, silently praying that Amanda wouldn't say anything too embarrassing.

"You wouldn't happen to have a brother, would you?" Amanda asked, giving Luc a once-over.

Mia inwardly groaned.

"Actually, I have four brothers."

"Jackpot." Amanda grinned.

Luc laughed. "Actually, I'm the best looking anyway. You'd throw rocks at my brothers."

"I'll take my chances," Amanda said.

"May I remind you that you already have a boyfriend?" Mia was amused.

Amanda shrugged. "I'm flexible in that regard."

"I'll keep that in mind." Luc laughed again.

"So, where's Beth Montaigne?" Amanda asked casually. "I'm a big fan of her lingerie."

Mia's heart began to beat faster at the mention of Beth. Why *wasn't* Luc with her?

"On the dance floor somewhere," Luc replied. "I'm sure she's surrounded by guys waiting for a dance with her."

"Why aren't you in that queue?" Amanda asked. "She's beautiful."

"She is, but we're just friends."

Amanda gave Mia a look, but she ignored it. Mia was embarrassed enough already.

Luc turned to Mia. "Can I talk to you for a moment in private?"

Mia blinked at him. She was feeling robotic again, unable to process her emotions in a timely matter. It was her default expression:

utterly blank. Yet her heart beat faster still and her hands shook a little.

"Sure," she managed to reply.

Amanda gave Mia a little push and winked at her. "Have a good time."

As they were walking away, Luc looked shyly at Mia.

"I hope your friends are having a good time."

"Maybe too much of a good time," Mia said. "Are any members of your family here tonight?"

"My little sister might come later in the evening," Luc said. "None of my brothers are free, even though I don't know why, given this is a lingerie store opening."

"That's too bad, although I'm sure having your sister here will make the night even more special."

"You're here," Luc said. "That already makes the night special."

Luc grabbed her hand. She hadn't expected it, or the kind words. His hand was warm, and she realized how cold her hand had been. Her heart pumped into the red zone.

"Where are we going?" Mia asked.

Luc took her down the hall, where the changing rooms were. They passed by floor-to-ceiling windows that pushed open like doors.

"Come on," Luc said.

The opening led to a small garden in the back of the store.

"It's beautiful out here," Mia said.

There was a rose bush, neatly trimmed hedges, and a small fountain in the center. It was dark outside, but the moon provided enough atmospheric lighting.

"Look, there's a full moon again," Luc murmured.

Mia looked up. Two moons ago, they had met. So much had happened since then, yet they hadn't changed, not that much. She was still the same woman Luc had met that night in Montmartre, and her good first impression of Luc still hadn't changed.

"What did you want to talk to me about?" Mia asked.

Instead of answering, Luc was looking at her with raw passion.

He kissed her. Softly at first. When she responded, he pressed his lips harder, leaving Mia breathless.

"I just wanted to see how that felt again," he said when they finally pulled apart.

Mia needed a moment to steady herself. The earth was moving like the sea, and she was still caught up in the tide.

"Luc," Mia said when she caught her breath. "What about Beth?"

He looked confused. "What about Beth?"

"Are you sure she's just a friend? I thought she was your girlfriend."

Luc shook his head. "She's not my girlfriend. Never was, never will be." He frowned, the blue of his eyes looking stormy under the moonlight. "Is that why you pushed me away? Because you thought I had feelings for Beth?"

Mia nodded. "I heard that you carried a torch for her for years, and there were rumors at the office that you went out on dates."

He arched an eyebrow, amused. "Oh? I always thought you were too intelligent to believe in rumors, Miss Golden."

"But Didier said that you were in love with Beth himself. I thought he'd know you better than anyone."

"Didier, huh?" Luc was still smiling. "Well, my business partner's an honest man. A man of his word. If he told me the sky had turned purple, I'd go outside and check. But for all his virtues, Didier does not have access to the contents of my heart. To give him credit, he was right. Past tense. I did carry a torch for Beth. I idealized her, but I didn't know her. A dream is only a dream when you wake up. Since I met you, I realized what love really is. It's when you don't even want to go to sleep anymore because reality is so much better. That's how I feel when I'm with you, Mia."

She couldn't quite believe what she was hearing.

"You're in love with me?"

Luc nodded, his blue-jean eyes locked on hers. "I have been since the moment I met you. You're just so alive, so full of guts, and you awakened a part of me that I never even knew was dormant. When you rejected me after the kiss, that really hurt. I accepted Beth's invite to dinner, thinking it would take my mind off things. It was just a dinner, and nothing happened. I still hold the opinion that Beth is a lovely woman. She has many good traits, and I'm sure a few negative ones, as all human beings do. She'll make a man very happy one day. The thing is, after getting to know her, I discovered that I simply didn't like her romantically. And I couldn't possibly have loved her because I simply didn't know her before. It was only infatuation."

"How does she feel about you? She must like you if she asked you to dinner."

Luc shrugged. "Yes, maybe she does, a little, but I doubt she'd miss me for long. She'll get over it. I'm sure one of her many admirers will whisk her off to the Maldives or the Bahamas, and she'll forget about me."

"You're not that forgettable, Luc."

His hand grazed her back, exposed by the open cut of her gown, and he felt that her skin was cold.

"Here, take my jacket."

He took off his black tuxedo jacket and put it around her shoulders.

Mia smiled and snuggled into his chest. She looked up at him again. "Why didn't you kiss me on the night we met? I thought we had a moment, and I felt so stupid when you pulled away."

"I was the stupid one. I kicked myself for being a coward. Literally. There were bruises on my shin." He shook his head. "I don't know. Men are generally stupid, and I belong in that sex. I wanted to kiss you, too, but the logical side of me kicked in, and I got scared. I'd just met you, and I was confused. But I regretted it. I devised a plan, you know, to see you again. Since I was too dumb to ask you for your number, I was going to work up the courage to swing by your apartment."

She giggled. "Were you going to raise your boombox over your head until I appeared at the window?"

"Something like that."

They could still hear the jazz band playing from the garden. They'd transitioned from an up-tempo number to a slow song.

Luc had his arms around Mia, and they slowly danced to the music.

"What about you?" Luc asked. "Are you in love with me?"

"Don't you know?"

"I do, but I want to hear you say it."

Mia smiled. "I started falling in love with you the night I met you, too. Then I tried to force myself to stop when I thought you were in love with someone else. Tonight, I can start loving you again."

And she would never stop.

"Good," Luc murmured. "I knew it. Kisses don't lie."

With that, he kissed her again.

CHAPTER TWENTY-FIVE

When Luc and Mia arrived at Parc de Villette, a large park in the 19th arrondissement, Les Slinks started playing the first song.

"Is that... Les Slinks?" Mia asked.

Luc nodded, grinning.

"I didn't know they were playing here," Mia said. "Is it a free concert?"

Luc was holding Mia's hand. It felt good to walk together holding hands. At the office, they had to maintain a professional distance, so when they were together out of the office, he never wanted to let her go. When they weren't together, he counted down to the time when he would see her again.

"Surprise," he said. "This concert is for you."

Mia's jaw dropped. "What? What do you mean?"

All he wanted to do was to make her happy, and he hoped she would be as soon as he told her what this was all about.

The park was crowded with fans dancing to Les Slinks' big hit song, "Beaux." Luc's brother was gyrating to the beat of the drums, then he began shouting into the microphone. Mathieu looked a lot like Luc, but with tanned skin and shaggier hair. The crowd sang along with him.

"I know you still haven't had much luck tracking down the woman in the Fizz commercial, so I figured I could bring some of that luck to you. The mystery woman came out to a free concert for Les Slinks once, even when the footage was going to be in a commercial, and I figured she would be a big enough fan to come out to another free concert. She was in the front row the first time. It meant she had come hours earlier to get that spot, so she must be a devoted fan."

"I can't believe you did this." Mia hugged him.

"It was about time I did something. You moved to Paris to find your sister, and I've been distracting you with a job and all the romantic dates."

Mia giggled. "But I didn't mind, especially the dates."

"My brother finally recovered from touring, so I figured why not force him to play one last show in his hometown before he starts recording for the next album? We rented out the space here and sent a blast to all the media outlets and social media two weeks ago telling them about this concert. I guess you must not be a Slinks fan if you didn't know about the free concert."

"I listen to Beyoncé," Mia said. "French alt-rock is not on my radar, I must admit."

Luc chuckled. "I figured as much. I don't listen to much rock either. It's funny how siblings can have such different musical tastes. My brother was the loudest person in the house growing up, but back then, we called it noise. It was annoying. But now he gets paid to make noise."

"It is quite loud," Mia said. "Even from back here. How are they not going deaf up in the front?" Mathieu was singing a refrain in French that Mia couldn't quite understand. "It is quite catchy, though. Do you really think there's a good chance my potential sister could be here?"

"If she's a big fan, she would've received the blast. The question is, would she have been able to make it to the concert? Today's a Sunday, and so I figured there's a good chance, if she's in Paris, that she's free to attend."

"True," Mia said. "Everything in Paris is closed on Sundays."

"We also ran a contest asking people to send in videos answering why they are the biggest Les Slinks fan. The winner gets a free trip to Paris to see them. If your sister wasn't in Paris, perhaps she would've sent in a video submission. Unfortunately, we went through the videos and none of them were her."

"Oh. Well, she could be from Paris."

"Yes, and we're also running another contest here, live. We've set up some cameras in the white tents over on the right side. See those tents there?" Mia nodded. "All the concertgoers are encouraged to enter the video contest. They have to look into the camera and tell Les Slinks why they love them. If they win, they get to meet Les Slinks backstage after the concert. We'd have their information and them on camera."

"You've thought of everything, haven't you?" Mia asked.

"We also have employees scouring the crowd looking for anyone who looks like you, just in case. They'll report to me if they do see someone who fits the criteria. So far, my phone hasn't rung, but there are over five thousand people here, and more are still coming."

"I can't believe you did all this for me." Mia hugged him again. "This must've been so expensive."

"You're worth it, Mia," Luc said softly. "I know how important this is for you."

She looked at him with such appreciation that Luc felt warm all over. "Thank you, Luc."

"Come on." He gently tugged her arm. "Let's go over to the contest tents."

"Hey, even if you don't find her from the contest videos, you can turn the submissions into a video montage of the fans and upload it onto Les Slinks' YouTube channel."

"That's a great idea," Luc exclaimed. "That's why you're a marketing genius."

As they walked across the park, which had been turned into an impromptu music festival, Mathieu had finished the first song and was now speaking to the crowd in French. Mathieu was giving appreciation to everyone who came to the concert, and the crowd erupted into cheers.

"I'm nervous," Mia said.

"Don't be. I'm here to support you."

A portion of the crowd had lined up to enter the video contest. Five cameras had been set up, managed by staff in black Les Slinks t-shirts. Luc observed the line. There was no one who resembled Mia, to his immediate disappointment.

"How's it going, Arthur?" Luc asked a young man who was in charge of the contest.

"Good. We've got around three hundred entries already," Arthur replied. "But nobody yet." He looked at Mia and switched to English. "You must be Mia, hello."

Mia gave him kisses on the cheek, as was the custom in France whenever you were introduced to someone. "Nice to meet you."

"As soon as we see someone who could be her," Arthur said to Luc, "we'll call you."

"Thank you so much." Mia's voice shook.

She also looked a bit emotional, and Luc took her to the side.

"What's wrong?"

"Nothing. It's just that I'm so overwhelmed. Everybody is here to help me, and you made it happen. Just the effort you've put in alone, I'll never forget it. You're so creative. I can't tell you how much I appreciate it."

Luc kissed her on the nose. "It's the least I could do. The Montaigne campaign is blowing the competition out of the water, the Damour campaign is also on fire, and now we've just landed the big Greek yogurt campaign. But I'm not doing all this because you've helped my company grow."

Mia's lips formed a playful smile. "So why are you doing it?"

Luc cleared his throat.

"It's because I love you, of course."

"I know. I just wanted to hear you say it."

"Don't I say it enough?"

"Yes, but I never get tired of hearing it."

"Well, I love you. Yes, even when you get impatient. Even when you eat off of my plate in restaurants. Even when you're so overly optimistic in this cynical nation. I love your crazy hair, your terrible French accent, your loud laugh. I love everything about you."

Mia laughed loudly, appropriately enough.

"Now it's your turn," Luc joked. "Why do you love me?"

Mia shrugged. "Some things are beyond reason."

At the unamused look on Luc's face, she broke out into laughter again. "Just kidding. What's not to love? You're handsome, you're smart, and you smell nice."

"That's all?"

"No, of course not. I love you for your soul. You have the most beautiful soul."

Mia's smile was so cute that Luc wanted to pinch her cheeks. Instead, he kissed her again, in the middle of the park, where Les Slinks were playing a slow love song, the perfect soundtrack to their romance.

CHAPTER TWENTY-SIX

*L*uc led the way to the V.I.P. section behind the stage. She was still in awe that Luc had put this concert together in less than three weeks. She hadn't even known about it. No man had ever gone to the lengths Luc had to prove how much he cared about her. She had to pinch herself. Was this really happening?

The V.I.P. section was another big white tent set up behind the stage. The decor was like that of a cocktail lounge. It was roped off from the rest of the park and guarded by security.

When they approached, a bouncer unhooked the velvet rope and let them in.

"Luc, there you are!" A young woman came over and hugged Luc.

"Audrey, this is Mia, my girlfriend. Mia, this is my youngest sister."

Audrey's blunt blond bangs made her look younger than her twenty-one years. She had dimples on both cheeks, and she looked petite and adorable in a green wrap dress and metallic sandals.

She greeted Mia with air kisses on the cheeks. "Luc has told me so much about you! Really. You're all he ever talks about all day long." She turned to Luc with a mischievous smile. "Am I embarrassing you, big bro?"

Luc shrugged. "Mia knows how obsessed I am with her."

"Must be terrifying." Audrey winked at Mia.

"Your brother is very sweet," Mia said.

"I have to admit he is. He's definitely the most romantic one in the family. He's the only one of my brothers who actually enjoys watching romantic comedies."

"Really?" Mia turned to him in surprise.

"I do," Luc admitted.

"He's seen them all. We have some really bad ones in French."

"I like the American ones too. If you must know, my favorite is *Hitch*."

"With Will Smith?" Mia asked. "The one where he coaches men how to behave on dates?"

"*Oui.*"

Mia laughed. "That's a good one. I've seen it at least twice."

"Now you know," Luc said.

"That's cute."

"Where are the others?" Luc asked Audrey.

As if on cue, two handsome men vaguely resembling Luc came into the lounge.

"Philippe, Xavier." Luc greeted them with hugs.

Philippe was still dressed in his white chef uniform without the hat. His light-brown eyes, dark hair, and soft, rounded features made him look sweeter than his more rugged brothers. Xavier looked like an athlete with his square jaw and sculpted body. He was an athlete in fact, a professional boxer in training. Dark gym clothes showed off every muscle, and he wore black-and-white Adidas sneakers. He was more tanned, like Mathieu, and his dark hair was shaved on each side of his head, giving it a short, mohawk-like look.

Luc introduced them to Mia. They both spoke English with charming French accents that were stronger than Luc's.

"I hear you're looking for your sister," Philippe said. "If she's as beautiful as you, I really hope we find her soon. Luc keeps telling me that you're the most beautiful woman in the world. I thought he might've been exaggerating, but now I see that he's right for once."

"Are you flirting with my girlfriend?" Luc half joked.

Philippe put both his hands up. "Just paying a compliment. It's what you do with beautiful women."

Audrey rolled his eyes. "My brothers all try to play the role of the seductive Frenchman. It's very cheesy. Don't buy it."

"Watch out for this guy." Xavier pointed to Philippe. "He's the ladykiller of the family."

"It's because he can cook," Audrey said. "That's why. Every woman likes a man who can cook."

Philippe grinned proudly, while Luc groaned.

"That means I have to spend more time in the kitchen with Philippe," Luc said.

Xavier laughed. "Luc can't cook for beans."

"Actually, Luc cooks okay," Philippe said to Mia. "Not as well as I can, of course, but he can make a decent ratatouille and a vegetable lasagna if he really follows the recipe."

"They're Mom's recipes," Luc added.

"Speaking of our parents," Audrey said, "they're in the country visiting our grandparents, so they can't make it after all."

"It's just as well," Luc said. "They've seen enough of Mathieu's concerts."

"It's probably better that Mom's not here," Xavier said to Luc and Mia. "She'll probably bug you two about getting married and giving her grandchildren as soon as possible."

Mia blushed. She didn't dare look at Luc. Their relationship was new, and they hadn't discussed the future yet.

"Mom still can't get enough of kids," Audrey said. "Sometimes I wonder if seven kids is enough for her. I'm the youngest, and she still babies me. I love her to death, but I'm moving into my own apartment as soon as I graduate, so she'll probably have empty nest syndrome. They were looking forward to meeting you, Mia. I'm sure we can all get together for dinner in the next few days. It's a little difficult to get everybody together at once, though, so we'll have to do without some people."

"Right," Xavier said. "Alain's on one of his work trips, and Madeleine's shooting a film in Prague."

"Meeting five out of seven Deneuve siblings is not bad," Mia said. "As soon as I meet Mathieu officially, that is."

Mia had been nervous about the idea of meeting Luc's siblings, but if the rest of the family were as easygoing and as welcoming as Audrey, Philippe, and Xavier, it would be a blast to spend more time with them.

Audrey was already chatting with Mia as if they were long-lost girlfriends. Philippe was a joker, and Xavier might have appeared to be a tough guy at first, but when he smiled, he looked like a cherub.

She chatted with them over drinks until the concert was over. Audrey told her a lot about the art history classes she was taking, how she was an artist, and what kind of paintings she was working on. They even made plans to visit the Montmartre museum to see some impressionist art.

Mathieu came in, all sweaty in his light-blue graphic t-shirt and ripped jeans. He was chugging down a bottle of water.

Luc waved him over. "Mathieu. I'd like you to meet my girlfriend, Mia."

Even though his face was flushed red and he was obviously tired from performing, Mathieu lit up when he greeted her. "So you're the one my brother's been so crazy about. I'm losing my voice because of you."

His voice was unusually hoarse. Screaming into the mic for an hour or two could do that to a person.

"Your voice is hoarse because you've been touring for the past three months," Philippe said.

"True," Mathieu said.

"Thanks for doing this," Mia said.

"No problem. I was thinking about doing a free concert for my fans anyway. Luc approached me with the offer to sponsor this concert, and I figured we can kill two birds with one stone. Any luck so far in finding your girl?"

Luc shook his head. "Not yet."

"But that's okay," Mia quickly added. "I was thinking if she doesn't show up today, we can always send your fans a link to my Facebook page. Maybe someone from your network would recognize her."

"That's a good idea," Mathieu said. "I can even write a letter to my fans myself."

"Really?"

"Sure. It's no problem. It'll be all over the Internet."

"Why didn't I think of this earlier?" Luc said. "You're a celebrity. Of course you can command that kind of attention. We didn't even need to put on this concert."

Mathieu laughed. "It's because you dream big. Simplicity doesn't suit you."

"So do you," Audrey said to Mathieu. "You weren't going to stop until you got to play in Madison Square Garden."

"And we did," Mathieu said. "But only as the opener for the Strokes. Next time, we'll headline."

"We all dream big in this family," Philippe said.

"A family of dreamers," Mia mused. "I like that."

"As you can see," Mathieu said, "the family is divided into athletes and artists. Xavier is the athletic one. Philippe too, when he's out of the kitchen and onto the soccer field."

"I have to work out," Philippe said. "Otherwise, with all the food I consume on a daily basis, I'd be pretty stout."

"Luc and I are the musical ones in the family," Mathieu said.

Mia turned to Luc in surprise. "How?"

"He sings too," Mathieu said.

"I have a fair voice," Luc said.

"More than fair. He's very good. When we were little, we sang in the church choir together, and they used to give him solos."

"Yes, but that was before I went through puberty and my voice changed."

"Oh, I don't know, I still think you have it in you." Mathieu turned back to Mia. "I keep asking him to duet with me on a record."

"Why don't you?" Mia asked Luc.

"I'm really not that good."

The chanting in the crowd got louder and louder.

Les Slinks, Les Slinks, Les Slinks.

"That's for you," Audrey told Mathieu.

"I have to go do an encore," Mathieu said. "Nice to meet you, Mia. See you guys in a bit."

Audrey, Xavier, Philippe, and Luc continued their conversation with Mia. They asked her a lot about her job as a journalist for *Seattle Life* magazine and the stories she used to work on.

"Mia writes great features," Luc said. "There was one that I read recently, about these parents whose daughter died from leukemia."

"That was a hard one," Mia said. "I kept having to go out and take walks when I was listening to the interview recording and trying to write it. I get really emotional when it comes to those types of stories."

"I'll have to read it sometime," Audrey said. "Are you planning to get back into journalism, to your old job at *Seattle Life*?"

Mia and Luc looked at each other.

"I don't know yet," Mia said. "I was supposed to go back to Seattle in eight months and take my position back."

Luc looked a little tense. He didn't say anything.

"We're just trying to enjoy the moment," Mia added. "See what happens."

"Of course," Philippe said, clapping his brother on the back in support.

"I think it's so wonderful that you have such a big family," Mia said.

"I hope you find your sister," Xavier said.

Audrey smiled. "Even if you don't, remember, you always have us."

The words touched Mia. She felt tears coming to her eyes, but she willed herself not to cry. Instead, she laughed and said, "Merci."

CHAPTER TWENTY-SEVEN

*L*uc had known that his siblings would like Mia. A couple of his brothers liked her a little too much, but who could blame them?

Even though their relationship was still new, he was hoping that Mia would change her mind and stay in Paris. He couldn't stand the thought of her leaving, but there was her job. Journalism was her first love. Mia wasn't going to stay in advertising forever. She had a real talent for writing, not to mention speaking to people, getting them to open up, and helping them tell their stories.

Mia was too good for advertising. He couldn't see her working at LUX forever. For the time being, it was a great experience for her. Advertising was a different way of telling stories and a fun creative outlet, but he wouldn't limit a woman with that many talents to offer the world to his own company.

Even with a lingerie campaign, Mia had found a way to shake things up, offer the public a different perspective on what a woman was supposed to be. The Montaigne campaign had received great feedback from the media and the public. He was especially happy to hear that young women were inspired by the ads. Mia, too, had been ecstatic to hear that. For Mia, touching people in a positive way was the reason behind everything she did.

He just hoped he could give her what she truly desired. Mia insisted that even if she didn't find the woman who could potentially be her sister, it would be all right. She had him and she had her friends, and of course her loving adoptive parents, but he discerned a sadness behind her eyes whenever she spoke about it. He didn't want her to lose hope. He'd just witnessed how much she enjoyed talking to his family and knew that she would be ecstatic if this woman turned out to be her sister.

As crazy as the Deneuve household had been growing up, he was lucky to be in a big, loving family. Not everybody had that. He was close with each one of his siblings. He had friends who didn't get along with their siblings at all.

Yes, he was extremely lucky to be surrounded by love. Now with Mia, the love had multiplied. The point of being surrounded by people you cared about and people who cared about you was to share love and grow together. There was nothing he wouldn't do for Mia and for his family.

Luc had been checking his phone throughout the afternoon, hoping one of his staff had spotted Mia's lookalike. No word yet. The concert was going to be over soon, and he had to fight himself to keep from being disappointed in order to stay positive for Mia.

There's still time, he told himself. *She could still be here.*

Mia was checking her own phone, and she seemed to be deeply absorbed in reading something on it.

"Are you checking your Facebook page?" Luc asked.

She nodded. "I've been getting a lot of messages lately. Five today, actually. Most of them are just supportive messages, wishing me luck. Sometimes they send links to people's profiles who turn out not to be the person I'm looking for. They mean well, but the info usually leads me to dead ends. But I just got this message in French. I still can't read too well. Can you translate it for me?"

"Of course," Luc took the phone. "It says, 'Mademoiselle Golden, I hope you're doing well. I was touched to hear your story, and I hope I can be of help. I'm one of the fiscal managers at the Paris branch of Prince Winterhouse, an international finance company. We work with a team of lawyers from the JJ Zower firm, and I believe the picture of the woman you posted is a lawyer from the team. Her name is Christine Moulin. She does have a Facebook profile under that name. I have not contacted her about this matter yet, thinking perhaps you might like the opportunity to contact her first. Thank you and I hope this helps. God bless. Sincerely, Marguerite Dumas.'"

"Oh my gosh." Mia put a hand over her mouth.

"Christine Moulin." Luc searched for her name on Facebook, and sure enough, a smiling picture of a young woman who bore a striking resemblance to Mia popped up.

"It's her. It's really her." Mia was amazed. She took the phone and zoomed in on her features. Then she clicked on her profile and read it.

"She does live here," Luc said, grinning.

"She's a lawyer, and I'm guessing from the years she attended school that she's around my age. She speaks fluent French, English, and German. Wow. She's quite accomplished."

"I expected nothing less, if she's your sister."

"Look, her top Liked page is Les Slinks. I wonder if she's here. Her profile's set to private, so I can't see her other information."

"Either way, you found her."

"This is amazing." Mia shook her head incredulously. "I can't believe it."

Luc was about to hug her when his phone vibrated in his pocket. Arthur was calling.

"Luc? You might want to come down here as soon as possible."

His heart was beating like crazy. "Why? You found her?"

"Possibly."

"Where is she?"

"She's in line for the contest with friends. You're lucky, because we were going to close the contest in ten minutes and announce the winners."

"We'll be there in two minutes." Luc hung up and grabbed Mia's hand. "She's here. She must've lined up for the contest right after the concert."

He led Mia out of the V.I.P. lounge, past the stage and the dispersing crowd, in the direction of the contest tents.

The line for the contest was longer than before, since Les Slinks had just finished their encore. The sun was at its peak, illuminating everyone. The crowd looked cheerful, having just enjoyed a free concert with one of the biggest bands in the country.

Luc spotted Arthur, and they ran to his side.

"She's there," Arthur said, "in the second line."

Luc and Mia craned their necks. They couldn't find her at first given the number of people.

Mia gasped.

She'd spotted her doppelgänger. Her light-brown Afro was tied back into what would've been a ponytail if it wasn't so fluffy that it became an automatic bun. She wore faded jeans, red-and-white–striped wedges, and a white crocheted top that was perfect for an outdoor concert. She was talking to a brunette and a pretty Asian woman, both in their twenties.

"I wonder if she's Christine Moulin," Mia said. "She has to be."

"Unless you have *two* potential sisters," Luc remarked.

CHAPTER TWENTY-EIGHT

"What am I supposed to say?" Mia panicked. "I'm shaking."

Luc put one of his strong arms around her shoulders. "Just tell the truth. Very simply."

She inhaled and exhaled, trying to calm herself down. The woman in line looked as if she was having fun, laughing with her friends. With the sun shining down on her, she looked like an angel, and it was hard for Mia to take in the fact that she was real.

"Look at her. She's so happy. She probably has a full life already. What if I become this huge... interruption in her life?"

"That's not possible," Luc reassured her. "You won't know anything until you talk to her.

She's right in front of you. You came all the way to Paris in order to find her. Don't talk yourself out of this moment. If she is your sister, she would want to know that you exist."

"I hope so."

Luc spotted the employees' cooler, and he took out a bottle of water for Mia.

"Drink this. It's hot. The heat's not helping."

"I'm gate-crashing her life." Mia let out a nervous laugh. She took the bottle and drank up.

"She won't mind." Luc's blue eyes shone. His voice was strong and masculine yet incredibly soothing. It put her more at ease. "You know why? Because a certain young lady crashed into my life not too long ago. I had plans, and you turned them upside down. In fact, my life has never been the same since then, and I don't ever want my life to go back to the way it was. What I'm trying to say is, you changed my life for the better. You owe it to that woman to do the same."

Mia knew that Luc was right. She looked back at Christine Moulin, or whoever this woman was. She was almost at the front of the contest line.

"I've always wanted a sister. I used to line up my stuffed animals and pretend that they were my long-lost brothers and sisters, and I used to make up my own stories about why my parents left me to reassure myself. The answers were out there, and I've been searching for them. Now that I'm a step closer, I'm afraid of finally knowing."

Luc pulled her in to him. "I know, *chérie.*"

His masculine scent was reassuring, and so was his warm embrace.

"I guess I'm scared that I'll be disillusioned by the truth. The perfect stories I've made up in my head will be shattered by reality."

"Mia, one thing I've learned since meeting you is that reality is better than illusions."

She looked up at him, tears welling in her eyes. He gently wiped them away with a thumb.

Mia had always thought she was an optimist, but in times of stress, the doubts descended. What if this woman didn't like her? What if they didn't get along? What if they had nothing in common? Christine was a multilingual lawyer who loved Les Slinks. Mia didn't listen to rock music, knew little about law, and was struggling to learn a second language.

What if Christine was one of those French people who despised Americans? Would she look down on her? She was a sophisticated Parisienne who had grown up with the Eiffel

Tower and the Louvre as a backdrop. Mia had the Space Needle. At least the cities had all that rain in common. But Christine probably didn't wear polka-dotted rain boots around Paris.

Knock it off, Mia told herself. This was not the time to compare French and American cultures.

Why did Luc always have to be right? The cowardly side of her was trying hard to talk herself out of approaching this woman. All her friends in Paris had conspired to help Mia, and she was not going to back out due to her own fears and insecurities.

"All right," she said with more assurance in her voice. "I'm going in."

She took another deep breath and started walking.

Mia's doppelgänger was still chatting animatedly with her friends. Her profile was to Mia. The trio of girls were speaking in rapid-fire French, but Mia knew that Christine spoke fluent English as well.

"Christine?" Mia said in a voice she hoped wasn't too shaky.

"*Oui?*"

The young woman turned around. The resemblance was so striking that Mia took a step back. It was almost like looking into a mirror. Her knees wobbled, and she wished she could hold onto something for support.

Christine's eyes also widened in shock. Her friends looked between Mia and Christine incredulously.

Mia felt shy. "Hi. My name is Mia Golden. I've been, well, searching for you. Do you mind if we speak in private for a moment?"

Christine looked back to her friends, as if for moral support. One of them nodded. The other looked stricken.

"Okay," Christine said, sounding just as shy.

The two of them walked to a patch of grass away from the crowd to talk.

"This is somewhat of a surprise to you, right?" Mia started.

"You look so much like me," Christine said. "How—?"

"I'll explain. I'm from Seattle, Washington. I was adopted at birth, and I never knew who my birth parents were, where I came from, or whether I had any blood relatives out there. Last year, I was watching YouTube, and a Fizz commercial came on. I noticed you, or someone who looks like you, in the video. That was you, right?"

"Yes. We heard Les Slinks were playing a free show. All we had to do was be extras in a commercial and get all the Fizz drinks we wanted. It seemed like a good trade-off."

"Well, I saw it, and I found out the commercial was filmed in Paris. It was incredibly difficult to track down who you were from a distance, so I moved here with the intention of finding you. Were you adopted as well?"

Christine nodded slowly. She still looked as if she couldn't believe the news. "Yes. By a French family. So you think we're..."

"Sisters. I know it's a lot to take in. I've had months to digest this information, but I understand if it's a shock to you."

Christine looked closely at Mia again. Her café au lait complexion had paled just a shade.

"I don't know who my birth parents were either, but I never thought I would have a living sibling out there somewhere. You're my long-lost sister?"

Mia smiled nervously. "I hope so. We'd have to take a DNA test. Is it okay if I give you a hug?"

"Of course!" Christine gave her a big bear hug. "We're sisters. I have a sister, a sister. I can't believe it."

Mia couldn't help but tear up. "I know. I have to pinch myself."

Christine cried as well. "We have the same hair, the same eyes... I didn't know someone existed out there who was like me."

They cried and hugged some more until they felt silly. Mia told her all about her adventures in trying to find her, including taking a job at the ad agency that produced the Fizz ad, Sarah creating the Facebook page, and the Slinks concert Luc had thrown just to help her find Christine.

"Your boyfriend must love you a lot," Christine said.

Mia turned around to see Luc smiling at her from afar. She smiled back. "He does. Oh, and Christine, you're the winner of the contest, by the way, along with your friends. You can meet Les Slinks."

"So the contest is rigged?"

"No, I suppose they will actually select five other winners randomly."

Christine laughed with tears still in her eyes. "I love Les Slinks, but meeting you is much better. I want to know everything about you."

"I want to know all about you too," Mia said. "Tell me everything. Even things you think are boring."

"Well, I grew up in the suburbs of Paris. My adoptive parents were going to adopt another girl from Vietnam so I could have a sibling, but the adoption fell through and I was an only child. I knew I was adopted from a young age, since I look nothing like my parents. We're a pretty typical middle-class family. *Papa* is in finance, and *Maman* used to be a ballet dancer, and now she operates a small dance studio. I do have extended family—cousins, grandparents, aunts—and I love them all. I'm the only adopted one in the family, however."

"So you were an only child, like me."

Mia told her about her parents as well, about her friends in Seattle, and her fondest memories growing up.

Christine invited her to meet her parents soon. Their house in the suburbs held Christine's childhood photo albums, which she was eager to show Mia.

"I would love to see them," Mia said. "My parents are visiting Paris for Christmas. You'll get to meet them then."

"This is just so crazy. When I woke up this morning, I never expected I would meet my long-lost sister. I don't think anyone needs a DNA test to know that we're sisters."

"Do you happen to have information on your—our—birth parents?" Mia asked.

"Not their identities, no. Do you?"

"No. I was thinking, maybe they just don't want to be found."

"That's what I figured," Christine said sadly. "I went through a phase of wanting to find them when I was a teenager, but if they don't want the information public, perhaps it just means they don't want to be found."

"It must be painful to give up your children," Mia said. "It might open old wounds if they did meet us."

"All the guilt that comes with it. I agree. It might be more painful for our parents, whoever they are."

Mia asked Christine her birth date. They had been born on the same day, which meant that they were probably fraternal twins.

The time flew as they caught up on the last twenty-seven years of their lives with each other. Their jobs, their first loves, their best friends, their passions. It started to rain, and the girls exchanged contacts.

Before Christine was scooted off to meet Les Slinks backstage, Mia gave her another hug.

"I'm so glad we met," Mia said. "I feel like I've just found the last missing piece of myself."

CHAPTER TWENTY-NINE

*H*is sister Audrey had been right when she said that Luc was the family's big romantic. He was not one of those men who dragged his feet when it came to marriage and commitment.

The real problem with romantic men was that when they were enamored with a woman, they idealized too much. Luc had made Beth out to be an unattainable goddess for a long time before he realized they were better off as friends. He had to be careful not to put Mia on a pedestal, too.

If he hadn't restricted himself, he would've proposed the week after they officially began dating.

Instead, he took his time in getting to know Mia. Being in love and starting a life together took more than romantic chemistry. They had to figure out whether they had the same interests, values, and goals in life. Enjoying each other's company was also important. Would they still enjoy spending time together for the rest of their lives? It was hard to imagine that they wouldn't.

His fingers were intertwined with Mia's as they walked along the Seine. When they walked across a bridge called Pont d'Iéna, which led to the Eiffel Tower, they could see the outline of the Sacré-Coeur church in the distance on their left.

"Look how beautiful the sky is," Mia pointed out.

The sun was setting, casting a rare pink-and-purple glow in the sky. Mia's childlike admiration for the beauty of the world made her even more adorable. She was the bright spot in his life. Everything she said either made him think or made him laugh.

After spending a few minutes with the other tourists admiring the tower, the sky, and their surroundings, they continued on their walk along the Seine. She admired the architecture of the buildings, pointing one out to him and saying how the textured facade reminded her of a honeycomb.

Being a Parisian, Luc was aware that Paris was a beautiful city. However, he took a lot of the city's beauty for granted, either by being immune to it or by not noticing it altogether. Mia's fresh perspective on Paris revived his own appreciation for the city. There was so much he wanted to show her, knowing that she'd appreciate it more than anyone. He loved to see her in awe.

Luc learned how to relax and seize the moment with Mia. Before her, life had been all about work and achievements, impressing others so he could feel like he was somebody. With Mia, he could be himself and be loved for it. It was easy to be with her. They could talk about anything as if they'd been best friends all their lives, and they could easily stay in comfortable silence in each other's company. Luc knew he was truly close with somebody if he could be silent around them and not feel the slightest bit awkward.

"You know," Mia said, "when I first came to Paris, I thought everything was so beautiful. Yet it was kind of lonely to be walking around all this beauty and not have someone to share it with."

"Paris does bring out the romantic in people."

"Yeah. It's as if every day is Valentine's Day here. If you have someone, it's the greatest, but if you don't, it can be lonely seeing all these happy couples walking around and making out all the time."

"True," Luc agreed. "I was so sick of those nauseating couples. Now we get to be one of them."

She chuckled. "Maybe I shouldn't blame Paris. I suppose I felt the same in Seattle too sometimes. I love cities where I can walk around. Walking helps me think and come up with ideas. It's inspiring. Sometimes I like doing it alone, and sometimes it's nice to have someone walk with me. Now that you're here, I have both options."

"Actually, this walking thing is new for me," Luc said. "I used to walk around Montmartre to get away from the craziness of my family, but that was years ago. Ever since I moved out on my own, it's just been rushing to the office or to meetings or to social gatherings. I rarely took the time to just walk and do nothing. I should make this a habit."

"You should." Mia sighed dreamily. "I hope I never fall out of love with this city. The moment I landed here, I felt this overwhelming support. There was a lot of good energy, a lot of love. Paris led me to you, and it led me to my sister."

"If you love this city and the city loves you, have you thought more about your job in Seattle?"

"Oh." Mia was quiet for a moment.

Her impending move back to Seattle was a sore spot for both of them. Mia only had a temporary work visa. While the job at LUX would've permitted her to renew her work visa for another year, Mia missed her career as a journalist.

"I don't know yet," she finally said.

They'd reached the beautiful Pont Alexandre III, a grand bridge lined with decadent sculptures and ornate street lamps. They walked to the middle of the bridge, where Mia looked down and watched the boats floating along the Seine. A tour boat was passing through, and the passengers waved up at them. Luc and Mia waved back.

"I don't want you to go," Luc said.

"I can't imagine being apart from you either," she said softly.

A smile slowly spread on Luc's lips. He reached into his coat pocket and pulled out a black velvet box.

"In that case"—Luc got down on one knee—"will you marry me?"

He smiled up at her hopefully.

Her beautiful features arranged into a look of pure surprise. A joyful surprise. Tears welled, and her hazel eyes glistened against the pink-and-purple sky light.

"Oh, Luc..."

She gazed at the ring. It was a princess-cut diamond surrounded by more tiny diamonds.

"I know it's only been a few months, but I know for certain that I want to spend the rest of my life with you. Mia, you know I mean it when I say that I want to make you the happiest woman in the world. I want to be the man who makes you happy."

"You already are." Tears ran down her cheeks, and her hands cupped her mouth. "Yes. Of course, I'll marry you, Luc."

He took the ring from the box and slid it onto her ring finger.

She gasped. "It's so pretty."

"I had my mother and Christine help me pick it out," Luc said. "If you didn't like this style, we had two backup options in mind."

"No, I love it. And look, it's a perfect fit, too."

She held her hand up, and the diamonds glistened.

"I know you'll miss your family in Seattle, but what do you think about living in Paris with me?"

"As your wife, I wouldn't dream of living anywhere else."

"Will you move into my apartment? You've seen it. It's big enough for two. You won't be living near Montmartre anymore, but we can visit my family's house there in case you miss the neighborhood too much."

"When I first met you," Mia said, "I thought you were a mirage, some kind of white knight on a black scooter waiting to save me. Now you're going to be my husband."

"A white knight?" Luc laughed. "You never needed saving. That's what I love about you. You can take me or leave me."

"But I want you."

"And I want you."

"My parents will miss me," Mia said. "But they are visiting for Christmas. This is perfect, because they can stay in my old Montmartre apartment. Maybe I can convince them to stay longer."

"And of course we'll visit them in Seattle."

"They're retiring soon. They might as well move here, even get to know Christine and her parents. I'm sure they'll have a lot in common." Mia laughed. "I'm getting ahead of myself. They do have some say in the matter."

"We'll see," Luc said. "I did ask your father for your hand over Skype, you know. They're ecstatic about visiting Paris. Maybe they will fall in love with France and move here."

"My mom has always talked about wanting to live in Provence when she retires."

"So it's a possibility. It'll all work out. You're moving in immediately, and we're getting married."

"My head is swirling," Mia said.

It began to rain. Drizzle. Details were important in Paris. "When you first met me," Mia continued, "that night in Montmartre, I was dancing, you know. In the rain."

"You mean before that mugger accosted you?"

"Yes. I was dancing by myself in the rain. And I'm not afraid to do it again."

"Here? In public? Now?" Luc shook her head. That was the thing about Mia. She wasn't afraid to be herself. She had fun without caring what other people thought.

"You can either watch me or join me. I'd prefer for you to dance with me, though."

Mia held out her hand. For Luc, it wasn't even a question.

He danced with his future wife on the bridge, in the middle of Paris, and he loved every second of it.

CHAPTER THIRTY

*W*hen Mia woke up, she was startled to see that it was almost ten a.m. She was going to be late for work!

But then she remembered: it was Sunday. And the bed she was sleeping in wasn't her Montmartre studio apartment; she was in Luc's king-sized bed in his apartment in the 2nd arrondissement.

Mia pulled away the fluffy white comforters, realizing that Luc's part of the bed was empty. Before she could call out for him, Tabby jumped onto the bed and meowed. Tabby was their new cat.

"*Bonjour, ma belle.*" Mia stroked Tabby's soft gray fur. "*Comment ça va?*"

Her French was coming along, slowly but surely. She was able to have basic conversations with people, but she still had a long way to go before she would be able to join in on conversations on politics and philosophy at French parties.

Christine had been helping her, speaking to her in French often so that Mia would be able to practice. She had to admit that she spoke a lot of English, especially with her friends from French class. If she was going to stay in Paris, she had to make more of an effort.

Sometimes she still couldn't believe that her life was real. When she had first come to Paris, she hadn't fully believed she would find her sister. Not only had she found her, she had also found the love of her life. As she drew back the curtains, her diamond ring glistened in the sun.

Married. She was married! It had only been a couple of weeks, being someone's wife. She still had trouble getting used to the idea.

It was a beautiful day, the sun's strong rays casting a heavenly glow over the whole room. Luc's apartment was in the thick of the 2nd arrondissement. They were on the top floor, and she could see into the gardens of the Tuileries.

Since it was Sunday and many shops and restaurants were closed, she and Luc planned on spending the day picnicking at the Tuileries for lunch and relaxing for the afternoon. At night, they were going to the Deneuve house in Montmartre for dinner, as they did most Sunday evenings. Luc's oldest brother Alain had just returned from his travels, and Mia was going to meet him for the first time.

Before she had gotten engaged, Mia had been at a crossroads about whether she would move back to Seattle when her year was up. She couldn't simply continue working at LUX as an employee, since she did want to go back to journalism, which was her true passion. It had been scary to consider giving it all up—the job, the city, and possibly the man—but she was glad she didn't have to make that choice.

Now that she was entitled to live in France, she could embark on her new career as a freelance journalist. Mia did have great relationships with editors from different newspapers and magazines, and she was sure there were plenty of stories to uncover and write about in Paris and in Europe. She had always had a natural flair for writing, and she was versatile when it came to topics. She already had a few story ideas to pitch, and she was in talks with an online Paris-based anglophone magazine about writing various articles.

She'd given Luc her two weeks' notice. Sarah, Amélie, and the other friends she'd made at LUX were going to miss her at the office, but it wasn't as if she wouldn't see them again. She could easily pop in at the office to say hi and have lunch with the ladies.

LUX was gaining more industry recognition than ever. Luc and Didier had even been nominated for a media award for the most innovative ad agency. She was tremendously proud of Luc.

"I need to get changed, Tabby." Mia placed the cat on the floor. "Why don't you go say good morning to Luc?"

Tabby ran out of the room, and Mia could hear her scuttling down the hallway. Mia changed out of her silk pajamas into her Sunday best: a yellow jersey dress and bright-orange patent flats. After she applied some simple makeup and tied her fluffy hair back with a gold leaf headband, she went out to the kitchen, where Luc surely was.

"Good morning."

Luc was in dark-blue jeans and a crisp light-blue dress shirt with the sleeves rolled up. He hadn't shaved that morning. He'd learned a month ago that Mia liked him rugged from time to time, and he took advantage of that when he didn't have to be clean shaven for the office.

His eyes lit up when Mia came in. She hugged and kissed him good morning.

"*Mon chou*," Mia said adoringly. "What does that mean again? My cabbage?"

"Hmm. It does sound strange when you translate it. It's like saying 'darling' or 'honey.'"

"My little cabbage," she teased. "That's what I'll call you."

"Little?"

"Oh, I'm sorry. I mean, my enormous cabbage."

Luc laughed. "That's more accurate." He put two plates on the table. "I went downstairs and got you the croissants you like."

"Yum," Mia said. "I really prefer this over..."

"Over my cooking?"

"Well, yes."

"Hey, those two hard-boiled eggs I made this week were legendary."

Mia shook her head with a smile. "Whatever you say. They were filling, at least. It's the effort that counts."

"In my defense, I was running late for work. This is why you shouldn't spend any time with

Philippe. The man makes up to twelve exotic dishes for breakfast when he's trying to seduce someone."

"He does sound dangerous," Mia said.

"Hey, at least I made fresh orange juice. That's got to count for something, right? Try it."

Mia drank up. "It's really good."

Luc looked proud, and Mia had to laugh. She was still the cook of the couple. Without her homemade food, Luc would be eating kebab takeout or dining all the time in restaurants. Nobody was perfect, and Mia certainly wasn't marrying Luc for his culinary skills. He was trying, however, and he was making an effort to cook more. In fact, he was going to go to the Deneuve house early to help his parents and Philippe prepare the dinner.

When Luc made the effort, he put his all into it. It was a trait that Mia respected and admired. They were going to be together for the rest of their lives, and Mia never wanted the spark to fade. She knew that marriage changed things for many couples. Once people got married, sometimes they stopped trying, but Mia would always cherish Luc.

They'd discussed having children someday. While they were not ready yet, Mia shared his excitement about becoming a parent. She'd come to Paris looking for a sister, a possible extension of her family. Not only had she found her, she was also going to begin her own family with Luc in the near future.

The past few months had been a whirlwind. If she stopped to think about it all, it made her head spin. Mia had never been so happy in her life, and it had all started at midnight in Montmartre.

ABOUT THE AUTHOR

Chloe Emile writes sweet, clean romance, whether it's contemporary or historical. She can usually be found working on her next novel, eating takeout with her husband, or watching rom-coms.

www.ChloeEmile.com

Chloe Emile